# The Doctor's Fake Fiancée

## A RED RIVER NOVEL

# VICTORIA JAMES

Entangled Publishing, LLC
2614 South Timberline Road
Suite 109
Fort Collins, CO 80525
Visit our website at www.entangledpublishing.com.

Bliss is an imprint of Entangled Publishing, LLC. For more information on our titles, visit http://www.entangledpublishing.com/category/bliss

Edited by Tracy Montoya and Alethea Spiridon Hopson
Cover design by Jessica Cantor

ISBN 978-1-50276-543-7

Manufactured in the United States of America

First Edition October 2014

*Bliss*

*I'm so happy to dedicate this book to all of my readers.*
*I feel truly blessed to have so many wonderful, supportive,*
*and thoughtful readers. You have all blown me away with*
*your emails, messages and comments. Whenever I receive*
*one of your emails or messages, it always makes my day.*
*I know I've kept you waiting for Evan's book-I hope you*
*enjoy this return to Red River and fall in love alongside*
*Evan and Grace.*
*A very special thank you to these readers: Stella, Kim,*
*Mandy, Monique, Nicola, Ellen, Jessica H, Christine P,*
*Marci, Pamela L, Ann, and Sandy.*

*Your most loyal fan,*
*Victoria*
*xo*

# Prologue

Grace Matheson needed to grow up. It was time to face the facts—she couldn't be a single mom, hold down a job, and pursue her dreams of becoming an artist. Her paintings weren't bringing in any money, so she couldn't afford to spend the time on them anymore.

"I promise it will never happen again. My babysitter canceled at the last minute, and I had no one to watch my son," she whispered into her phone. Her eyes focused on the road ahead and she cringed as the office manager gave a long sigh on the other end of the line.

She cursed herself for staying awake almost the entire night to finish a painting. When she'd finally stumbled to bed at five in the morning, she'd forgotten to set her alarm and had woken up two hours late for work, in a complete panic.

"Grace, this is the last time. I think you're a very nice person, but I need a reliable receptionist in Dr. Harris's office. One more chance. We'll see you tomorrow, okay?"

# The Doctor's Fake Fiancée

"Thank you, Cynthia." She breathed a long sigh of relief, easing her foot off the gas as she approached the turnoff to the highway. Her heart squeezed painfully as she glanced in her rearview mirror at her son, who was sleeping soundly. Being a single mother was harder than she ever could have imagined, and she'd naively thought she could juggle everything, including her son. Christopher had never been planned, but there wasn't a doubt in her mind that he was her first priority.

She looked away from the mirror to the road ahead, just in time to see the eighteen-wheeler take the highway on-ramp too fast. Her heart slammed up against her ribs with the painful realization that she wouldn't be able to get out of the way in time. She pounded the brakes and veered the steering wheel to the left.

Her car, the truck, the road, blurred and slowed until they floated in only a silent, throbbing bubble. The ominous, thunderous drone of the truck turning on its side and slamming onto the road, mingling with Christopher's shrill cry, were the last sounds she heard before everything turned black.

• • •

Voices, no, *a* voice was calling her. Where was she?

"I'm going to get you out of here, sweetheart. Can you hear me?" the person said again. It was a man's voice. It was familiar. It was gruff, strained, and filled with…worry. She tried to lift her head to nod, but it was as though she were trying to lift a sandbag. Sirens hummed in the distance, slicing through the fog that held her mind captive.

"Mommy," a little voice whimpered, a voice that she knew instinctively, that kicked her adrenaline into high gear.

"Christopher," she tried to yell, but she could only manage a soft whisper. She needed to get to her son.

"He's fine. He's going to be okay. I'm a doctor," the man said. The reassurance was all she had to cling to. There was shuffling. Christopher was whimpering, and she struggled to push against whatever it was that was pinning her down.

"Where are we?" She tried to blink, but whenever she opened her eyes, they burned. She squeezed them shut and tried to breathe, but her lungs were heavy. Smoke. There was smoke.

"You were in a car accident. Help is on the way. I've got you and your son almost out, okay? I need you to stay calm and just do as I say. I'm not going to let anything happen to you," the man said. His hands reached across her waist, and she felt him tug. Strong arms moved across her body as he pulled at the seatbelt. There was something about him, a familiarity. She tried to stay awake, to open her eyes, but it was useless.

"The car is filled with smoke, and that truck is going to light up. We've got to get out of here. Can you move?" He continued to pull the seat belt. Adrenaline and panic raced through her, and she prayed for strength as she tried to move, to lift her limbs. Nothing moved. Or worked.

"Mommy," Christopher cried and then coughed. He needed to get out of the car. She needed to save her baby.

"Christopher, it's okay, Mommy is here," she said, willing her voice not to waver. The man's head hunched close to hers. "Just get my son out, okay? I'll be fine. Get him out," she pleaded.

"I'm getting you both out," the man said, his voice rough and sure. There was strength in it.

"Get him out. Promise me—"

He ignored her plea and pulled on her seat belt again. It finally unlatched, and she felt his sigh of relief. "Got it. I want to wait for the paramedics to get here before I move you, but I don't know how long we have. Your car is sitting right under the truck."

Panic swam through her body. The smoke grew thicker, and she began coughing. Everything ached, and she fought desperately to stay awake.

"I'm going to get you out of here, sweetheart," the man repeated, and there was that comfort in his voice, something that made her want to believe him.

Maybe she could close her eyes for a minute. Just a minute.

Seconds later, minutes later, hands were lifting her. People were talking. She listened for the man. There were different voices. Something about a fire. And getting out. Grace struggled to break through the fog in her head and the sleep that was drowning her, the heat that was stifling her ability to speak. Christopher. Where was Christopher? The man?

"Christopher," she tried to yell as her body landed on something soft and cool.

"He's coming," a woman said as she placed something hard against Grace's neck.

Her son's shrill, distraught scream, mingled with a man's roar of pain shot through the haze she was engulfed in. Her eyes sprang open, and a striking blaze of orange was all she saw until darkness claimed her.

# Chapter One

Dr. Evan Manning hung up the phone and cursed loudly inside his empty office. There was no way around it: if he wanted to restore his position at the top, he needed to find a wife. Or fiancée. By next week.

But first he was going to have to deal with a full day of patients. He scowled at his computer screen and fought the urge to jam his fist in his mouth. His eyes glazed over as he read the roster of upcoming appointments:

9:00 a.m. — Eunice Jacobs: Toe fungus

9:20 a.m. — Crystal Boon: Warts

9:40 a.m. — Jeremy Morris: Hemorrhoids

He stopped reading and dragged his hands down his face with a loud groan. There was precisely one month left of this monotony. These were the kind of medical issues he'd never had to deal with in the ER. There was no adrenaline rush in prescribing hemorrhoid cream and more fiber. When his mentor, the doctor that he'd admired as a child and had stayed in close contact with professionally and personally, had suffered a mild heart attack and had asked Evan to fill in for him for a month to six weeks, Evan had readily agreed. The timing had been ideal, really. He was about to make a major career move, and the dead-crawl pace in Red River would give him the extra time to ensure he got what he was after.

But small-town, family practice was definitely not what he'd expected: it was much worse. People in Red River were all about long conversations and getting into everyone else's business.

A short, quick rap on the door reminded him that he was a professional, and small-town horror or not, he had a job to do. He composed himself and swiveled on the worn chair to look at Sheila, the receptionist standing in the doorway. Her tightly curled gray hair seemed to stand on end as she frowned at him. He attempted a smile, but her glower only deepened. He took a deep breath and pretended he was a patient man.

"Dr. Manning, this is my official notice of resignation," she announced with a huff, walking forward and slapping a letter on his desk. He tore his gaze away from her angry face to the envelope on his desk. He had been here less than a week, and the receptionist of almost thirty-five years was quitting.

"Sheila, you can't resign—"

"I *can,* and I *will*. You may be easy on the eyes, young man, but I'm past the age where my hormones will respond to those baby blues of yours. In all my years working with Dr. Chalmers, I have never been so patronized or overworked—"

"I didn't patronize you. I know you're an invaluable part of this practice. As for being overworked, I'm sorry, but I just noticed that there were many files and systems that needed updating. I thought it would be nice to get this place up to speed before Dr. Chalmers returns from his sick leave." Actually he thought the way this entire place was run was archaic and without any kind of discipline. Judging by her herculean stance, she wasn't in the mood to be criticized.

"Well, I do not appreciate working under a dictator. Maybe this kind of thing is acceptable in the city where you're barking out orders in the ER, but this is Red River. Here we take the time to say good morning and ask about your family and talk about the weather. I will remind you, Evan Manning, that I knew you when you were running around in diapers, trying to keep up with those older brothers of yours." She paused for a moment, and he sincerely hoped it was the end of her tirade. But then she puffed up her chest, and he braced himself. "You were much sweeter then."

For chrissakes. The constant reminders that everyone knew him when he was a child drove him nuts. He'd been back for all of one week, and he was ready to enter the witness protection program to ensure no one would ever find him again. Her voice screeched on, and he glanced over at his computer display, wondering if there was a way he could switch the screens and get to his email account without Sheila noticing. He nodded seriously at her, when he heard the words "settle down," and slowly placed his hand on the mouse, his eyes not leaving hers. And then she swatted him with a medical file.

"Are you even listening to me? This is what I'm talking

about—I refuse to work for a person who can't even be bothered to make eye contact with me."

He looked at her, squarely. "I have been listening to you."

Her eyes narrowed to little blue slits, and he braced himself for another unsolicited opinion. "Do you know what's wrong with you, Evan Manning?"

Sheila seemed to think that because she and his mother had been friends, and that she'd seen him in diapers, she was qualified to give him life advice. He stretched his legs out in front of him, forcing his muscles to relax and his mind to numb. "Please tell me, Sheila. What's wrong with me?"

"You need a wife. A family."

Exactly right. Had she been eavesdropping on his phone conversation? When his Good Samaritan stint in Red River was over, he would hopefully be on his way to running North America's most exclusive plastic-surgery clinics. All he needed in order to seal the deal was to convince the head of Medcorp that Evan Manning was a family man, the ideal choice to oversee the network of clinics for the wealthy, family-owned company. Then his career would be back on track. Sure, his surgery days were over after the accident, but he'd be at the top again. And that was the most important thing.

*You need to be the best. You are bigger than this small town. Don't disappoint us, Evan, not like Jake. Stay focused on your goals.* Evan frowned. He hated when his father's voice popped into his head without warning. Especially since he now knew the truth about his father.

"Well," Sheila prodded, effectively drowning out his father's voice.

"Maybe you're right. So why don't you stay, point out my flaws, and then when the month is up, you can go on vacation? Just think, how will Dr. Chalmers feel when he returns to find that you've retired? I'm only here for four more weeks. He'll be recovered and back at work, and I'll be in Toronto—I'll be nothing but a memory to you."

"More like a nightmare," she said, her chest inflating like a rooster again. "I'm sorry, but I'm leaving. Life is too short to be wasted here. I've booked myself a Mediterranean cruise. I have left instructions and detailed notes on my desk for whatever poor, unsuspecting receptionist you coerce into taking my place. So, as the Italians say, 'adios.'"

Evan rubbed the back of his neck, and flipped open the file. "Actually, it's 'ciao' or 'arrivederci.'"

"Excuse me?"

He flipped through the file and nodded. "The Spanish say 'adios.' The Italians say, 'ciao' or 'arrivederci.'"

Sheila let out a choked sound and then whirled on her beige, rubber-soled shoes and marched out of the small office.

Dammit. So now, he needed a receptionist, a wife, and a freaking prescription for high-blood-pressure medication.

Five minutes later, Mrs. Jacob's high-pitched squeal rattled the silence of the small office. Good *God*. This was going from bad to catastrophic. Evidently, Sheila hadn't bothered to lock the door behind her. He was going to have to get through this day without a receptionist.

He pulled out Mrs. Jacobs's chart as her heavy footsteps approached at a rapid, ominous pace and stood, the sudden movement causing his swivel chair to glide across the spotless linoleum floor and bang into the examination table.

He tried to mentally prepare himself for the inevitable on-slaught of nonsensical questions from the elderly woman. He opened the door, ready to face the most eccentric pa-tient of the day, only to have her barrel though the door like a bushel of apples.

"Dr. Evan," Mrs. Jacobs huffed, lunging forward and forcing him to back up a step. Eunice Jacobs was probably the only person in Red River who called him Dr. *Evan* in-stead of Dr. *Manning*—and the only person to wear a rain-coat in sunny weather.

"Good morning, Mrs. Jacobs." He took another caution-ary step backward, needing a healthy dose of space between him and the woman who smelled like rancid garlic. He forced himself to look down at her foot, which she had raised from the ground and was dangling in the air. He stifled his need to curse and grabbed her arm to steady her as she seemed precariously close to losing her balance. Her pink, sparkling sandals were looking more stuffed than a turkey on Thanks-giving.

"I jammed some disinfectant around the nail, added fresh garlic, and wrapped it in gauze. But you need to fix it so that I'll fit into my stilettos for my wedding next Saturday."

He bit down on his tongue so hard he worried he cut it. He had no idea how this woman thought she'd ever get those wide feet of hers crammed into stilettos.

"And where is dear old Sheila?" she continued. "I had much to discuss with her this morning!"

Evan cleared his throat. "It seems she planned a vacation and decided it was time to retire." He coughed. "Today."

Mrs. Jacobs frowned. "That doesn't sound like Sheila. And she had confirmed she was coming to the wedding.

Hmph." Mrs. Jacobs plunked herself down on a chair with a massive sigh. "Now I do have to apologize in advance that I won't be able to stay and have a little chat. Lots to do these days; it's wedding time!"

Jeez. This was small-town family practice. *Chats?* There were no *chats* with the doctor. No wonder Chalmers could never keep to the ten-minute appointment slot Evan had tried pressing Sheila to convert to. No, Chalmers had people booked in twenty-minute slots. Twenty minutes with Eunice Jacobs would make *him* retire early.

He tried to concentrate on the examination of her foot, but his mind was on his current issues. He needed a receptionist. *Today.*

Tomorrow he could worry about finding a wife.

• • •

Grace pulled the key out of her car ignition, and the engine sputtered and coughed until it was completely silent. She said a silent prayer that it would actually start up again and get them home to Toronto. This car was on its last leg, and she knew for certain that she would soon be relying on public transit. Which might be for the best considering the cost of gas these days.

She glanced in her rearview mirror at Christopher, who was still asleep. The three-hour car ride from Toronto to Red River had been filled with nonstop questions, complaints, and one washroom stop. She was partly to blame, because they could have arrived a lot quicker if she'd taken the highway. But she hadn't been on one since the accident. Instead she'd mapped out a route comprised only of country back roads. It had been picturesque—for the first hour. Then the farms and cows and sprawling countryside had lost their appeal to her four-year-old son.

She leaned to one side and peered through the passenger window at the little white house. It was on a tree-lined side street, downtown Red River. At one time it must have been someone's home and then converted into an office. There was a white, painted wooden sign perched in an immaculately kept garden bed on the front lawn that read DR. CHALMERS FAMILY PRACTICE.

Grace drew a long, unsteady breath and then glanced at the Spider-Man notepad sitting beside her on the passenger seat. She opened it and flipped through the pages until she reached today's to-do list. To-Do lists were "her thing." She made one for every single day, no matter how big or small the day's events were going to be. Sometimes she added even the tiniest items so she'd feel more accomplished. To-Do lists made her think of her mother—Grace remembered her mother making one every day. *A single mom's necessity*, she'd say under her breath.

Grace dug through her crappy bag that was on the brink of self-destruction and felt around for a pen. The only thing she could find was an orange crayon. Good enough.

She studied the remaining items on today's list:

*Drive to Red River*
*Meet Dr. Manning (don't act like an idiot)*
*Give Dr. Manning present (don't forget Christopher's gift)*
*Thank Dr. Manning profusely*
*Drive home*
*Job Interview (don't screw it up)*

She crossed out the first item on her list with the crayon. Then she clenched it in her sweaty palm and took a deep breath. This is where she would find Dr. Evan Manning. He was the man who'd saved her and Christopher. It had taken her over a year to track him down, and last week, by some stroke of luck, she'd stumbled across information about him. She'd been at the emergency room in Toronto General, because Chris had sprouted a high fever in the middle of the night and she'd rushed him to the hospital. The doctor who'd treated him for a double ear infection was asking about the scars on his body, and she ended up telling him about the car accident and the mystery man who'd saved them. As luck would have it, the doctor was a colleague of Evan Manning and knew all about Dr. Manning's heroics that day. The doctor told her Manning was temporarily working in his hometown of Red River.

Grace had seen the conversation as a sign. She needed to thank the man who had saved their lives. She baked a batch of their favorite cranberry muffins and wrapped them up in cellophane with a big red ribbon. And Christopher had spent an entire hour drawing his hero a picture.

"Chris," she whispered, turning in her seat to look at her son. He stirred slightly, his dark hair rumpled. She smiled at the sight of him, his faded Spider-Man shirt hugging his thin frame. He'd insisted on wearing it, explaining his logic that he should wear a superhero, since Evan Manning was one. "Come on, honey, time to wake up; we're here."

She turned to the front and collected her keys, dragging her hands down her face as she caught a glimpse of herself in the rearview mirror. If Ronald McDonald had an older, crazier-looking, dark-haired sister, she'd be her. Except

Grace probably looked even worse, because she didn't have the access to that kind of heavy makeup.

She attempted to smooth down her curly hair but, when that didn't work, frantically searched her purse for something to tie it back with. She chewed her lower lip as she held a Spider-Man shoelace in between her fingers. It could work. No one would notice if she wrapped it tightly. Working quickly, she finger-combed her curly hair into a high ponytail. And then frowned at her reflection. Well, whatever. Good enough. It's not like she was here to pick up Evan Manning and impress him with her looks…or lack of. She was here to thank the man. Profusely. He'd saved the most important person in the world to her. Her concern over her pathetic appearance seemed trivial in comparison to the real issues they faced.

Christopher yawned loudly. "Where's Dr. Nevan?"

"Dr. *Evan*. I think he's inside. Ready to go?"

Her son stretched and then bopped his head up and down quickly. "I've never met a real live superhero."

Grace stifled her groan as she opened her door. The superhero fixation was reaching new heights and showed no signs of slowing down. She helped Christopher out of the car, and they held hands as they walked up the flagstone path to the front porch.

The small waiting room was empty when they entered. Grace frowned as they stood in the doorway. It was odd for a doctor's office to be so quiet. The practice she'd worked at for years had always been bustling, and phones were always ringing—even when it was closed. Maybe this was what small-town family practice was like. The cellophane crinkled as she balanced the plate of muffins on her hip and walked toward a French door that separated the waiting room from what must be the examination rooms. She winced at the loud creaking of the old door but walked through anyway.

They could hear a man's deep voice speaking, filling the otherwise-quiet space. She stopped hesitantly outside the first room, Chris bumping into her. Seconds later, the man said good-bye and hung up the phone. Her heart hammered incessantly as she waited for him to turn around. When he didn't, she cleared her throat and knocked on the door.

The man turned in his chair and slowly stood. He must recognize her.

Her mouth went dry as she stared into his striking blue eyes. Everything was arresting about the man. Perfectly chiseled jaw, high cheekbones, and a mouth that was somewhere between sensual and severe. A few strands of gray visible amidst his thick, dark hair. She noticed the outline of the broad shoulders, tapering to a narrow waist and long, lean legs.

Good God, she was checking out their unbelievably gorgeous rescuer.

And she was dressed in pregnancy jeans with a Spider-Man shoelace holding her Ronald McDonald hair up.

# Chapter Two

Evan stared at the woman who'd been in his mind, his memories, for a year.

The same woman he'd saved from a car wreck.

When he'd run to the car that was filled with smoke, he'd had no idea what condition the occupants would be in. His heart had stopped, seeing the woman lying motionless, her face bloody as he climbed into the car. Adrenaline had kicked in. And when he saw the little boy in the backseat, something in his gut had propelled him to work faster, harder. Failure hadn't been an option. But he'd been seconds too late, and now he was left to deal with the repercussions. His injured hand clenched in his pocket. His girlfriend and fellow surgeon, Alexandra, had left him, disgusted that his career had to be put on hold due to his injuries and they were no longer professional equals.

In the hospital, during his grueling recovery, he'd have nightmares of the woman and her little boy. He'd dream they both died. He'd hear their cries mixed with his. The staff at the hospital he'd been sent to reassured him the woman and child were fine. That was all he needed to know.

He allowed himself a rapid perusal. Emerald eyes, dark hair, full red lips. Her shiny hair was disheveled, in a heap on top of her head. And her clothes were frumpy. Jeans that disguised her shape were swallowed up by an oversize dark jacket. But her face was undeniably beautiful. No amount of cheap, poorly fitted clothing could hide that. When her gaze met his, he felt a jolt deep in his gut. He glanced down at the little boy holding her hand. He had a mop of wavy, dark hair and judging from his height was probably around four years old. Evan's hand curled around the medical chart, gripping it tightly. He swallowed past the lump in his throat as the child looked up at him. He'd never forget those eyes. They were deep green, identical to his mother's, and Evan was struck by the memory of him trapped in that car seat. Or maybe it was because he still felt the imprint of the little boy's fists against his shoulders as he pulled him out of the car, seconds before it had burst into flames, the explosion knocking them to the ground.

The woman cleared her throat. "Are you Dr. Evan Manning?"

He nodded and crossed the room. The kid was looking at him with pupils that had taken on a comically large size as he walked toward them.

"Oh, Dr. Manning, my name is Grace Matheson, and I have been looking for you for over a year. I cannot begin to thank you for what you did—"

The kid lunged forward, looking like he couldn't fully control his limbs. "You're a superhero—"

"Shh, Chris." Grace grasped the back of his shirt, reining

him in. "I can't believe…I don't know what would have happened to us if you hadn't saved us."

They'd be dead. Not that he could say that aloud. Especially not with the little boy in the room.

Her son tugged at her arm. "Give him my picture."

"Oh right. Here, Christopher drew this," she said with a hesitant smile. She thrust a drawing at him. Evan looked down at it, frowning. He had no idea what the giant blob of red and yellow was supposed to resemble. He eyed the little boy and then cleared his throat. "This is, uh, really some nice work you've got here."

The kid beamed. In fact, he looked like a piñata, ready to burst. Then the Grace woman shoved a crinkly package at him. "I baked these for you. They are Christopher's favorite muffins—"

"They're sooooo good. You'll love 'm! Try one!"

"Chris, maybe Dr. Manning doesn't want a muffin right now," she whispered.

Evan shot the boy a smile. He didn't know what the hell to say to these people. "Thanks. You didn't have to do all this." He gestured to the picture in one hand and the muffins in the other. He placed them on the examination table. He felt… odd. Touched. As an ER doctor and surgeon, he didn't really have to form relationships with patients. And in his personal life, he never dated women with kids. And Alexandra hated anyone remotely resembling a child. Kids had never really been in the cards for him, so he always found himself kind of awkward around them, like they might call him out on the fact that he didn't know what he was doing. The only two that had ever had a hold on him were his niece and nephew. Luckily for him, they probably assumed his weirdness was due to the gene pool he shared with their fathers.

"Are you going to eat one?"

This kid was persistent. "Not right now, but as soon as I have a second, I'm sure I will."

The woman was frowning slightly, pulling her full lower lip with her teeth. It was a nice lower lip. Not that he should be noticing. He forced his eyes up.

"I'm sorry that we burst in here without warning. I had just been searching for you for so long, and I couldn't go on thinking that the man who'd saved us never even had a thank-you. Christopher had the day off school and I...well, I didn't have anywhere to be this morning, so I thought it was the perfect time to come out here and say it." Her dark green eyes locked with his, and something stirred in him. It must have been the earnest way in which she spoke. There was no bullshit, no agenda, just simplicity. And his lackluster welcome was obviously now making her embarrassed.

He gave her a slight nod. "I'm just glad it all turned out okay."

Her smile faltered and what looked like disappointment flickered across her face. He didn't know what she'd been expecting, but he could tell he wasn't delivering it.

"Well, we'd better get back to Toronto." she said, backing up and tugging her son along. "I, uh, have a job interview later this afternoon." She retreated a few more steps until she bumped into the door, her cheeks gaining color.

Politeness dictated he at least feign interest. And he didn't want to be an ass. They had gone out of their way to thank him, even though he hated talking about the accident that had killed his career. "What line of work are you in?"

"My mom's an artist!"

She smiled down at her son. "Well, actually I just do that in my spare time. I'm really a medical receptionist."

He blinked, everything pausing for a moment before a plan appeared in his mind, complete with a time line and details. Seriously? He glanced down at her left hand. No ring. Single mom.

He looked out the window, zeroing his gaze on what had to be Grace's car parked outside the clinic. It was a clunker. He turned to her, taking in the shabby clothes. Jobless or close to it. His heart sent blood rushing to his head. This could happen. This Grace woman and her son could be just what he needed.

He cleared his throat. "I'm actually looking for a receptionist."

Her mouth dropped open. "Oh. Wow. Well, thank you, but the commute from Toronto every day to here would be too much."

He nodded, thinking of a way to do this. He wasn't a manipulator by nature. But life had handed him some pretty crappy luck lately, and he needed to find his way back to the top. There was no way in hell he'd let that position at Medcorp go to someone else while he withered away in a small-town family practice. "Right. Too bad. Would have been quite the coincidence. You helping out the man who saved you…"

Her chin wobbled, ever so slightly, and he shrugged off the guilt he felt for manipulating. "I mean of course, I could never repay you for what you've done, and I would love to help you out. I just don't know how I could drive from Toronto to Red River every morning and night. And Chris is in kindergarten."

"I don't know anything about your circumstances, but this job starts immediately. The pay is excellent, and the cost of living in a small town is much less than Toronto."

She frowned slightly. "Chris, why don't you do some coloring over there," she said pointing to the exam table and handing her son a book and crayons from her enormous bag. Christopher nodded and grabbed everything into his arms and then spread it all out on the examination table. Evan stifled his irritation that he'd now have to change the paper on the table before the hemorrhoid patient came in.

He turned to Grace and took a few steps closer to her. That's when he noticed the depth of color in her eyes. The gorgeous, full lips. Flawless skin. He swallowed hard. He hadn't had luck like this fall into his lap in...ever. This could work.

At the end of it, she'd get a new job and free living expenses for a few months. He knew exactly where she could live, too. Of course that would mean involving his brothers, but he was pretty sure they'd agree. Knowing them, they'd think it was a sign he was settling in Red River for good. He'd deal with his family's disappointment later. Because other than that, it was the perfect plan. Really, he shouldn't be feeling guilty at all. What he was about to do was practically saint-like. Then he and Grace could go their separate ways. What could go wrong?

Her voice dropped to a whisper. "Um, that's really sudden—"

"I could put you up in a house, all expenses paid, and of course you'd be very well compensated for your work here."

"This sounds too good to be true." She crossed her arms and looked him up and down. She was looking a little less sweet, a little less meek. "Why would you do all this for me? You don't know me; you don't even know if I'm really even a medical receptionist—"

He tried to look as calm as possible. The last thing he wanted was to freak her out and send her running. "Do you have a résumé? References?"

She nodded slowly. "In my car. So this is full-time work, with benefits…and a place to live?"

He nodded, waiting for that to sink in.

"How do you know I'm not married or have a boyfriend or other ties to Toronto?"

Crap. "I just assumed because you weren't wearing a wedding band—"

"You're right. Okay, well… Are there any other things I should know about this position?"

He glanced over at her son, making sure he was still coloring, and then lowered his voice. Well, he'd better get the rest of his plan out there. "The only other job requirement is that you pretend to be my wife."

• • •

Grace stared at the most handsome man she'd ever met. The man who had saved their lives, and she wondered if he was insane. He didn't give off creepy, stalker-murderer vibes, but still, a woman could never be too careful. She glanced over at Chris and didn't even bother telling her son not to draw on the actual paper on the table and to keep it to the books. She couldn't because right now, this Dr. Manning was telling her he needed a wife.

She cleared her throat. Maybe it was a joke. *Obviously*

it was a joke. He was joking and had an odd sense of humor. "That's funny, I thought you just said you 'need a wife'?"

He gave her a nod. "Or fiancée. Maybe that would be easier to spin, actually."

He was not joking. Those sky-blue eyes of his didn't have an ounce of laughter in them. "I'm not following this," she whispered. "You need a secretary, slash, wife, slash, fiancée?"

He nodded again. "Right. It's fake. Just for a month. All I need you to do is attend a few social events with me. But the receptionist job is yours to keep. I'm only here for a month, and the doctor who normally runs this clinic will need a secretary."

"Are you sure you can't find someone else willing to attend a few social functions with you?"

"I need someone that no one in my usual circles knows."

"What kind of a job would make you have to fake a wife?"

His jaw clenched, and a shadow passed over his eyes. "It's a position to head up a new set of medical clinics that are owned by a company with strong family values. No one said that I *have* to have a wife. But a good friend of mine on the inside told me that the frontrunners for this position were all married with children—and that was intentional on the part of the people doing the hiring. I'm not willing to lose this opportunity because I don't have a wife."

It all sounded surreal and like a lot of trouble to go through just for a job. She didn't need someone else's problems in her life. She had more than enough on her plate. "This sounds deceitful—"

"Grace," he whispered in a voice that was deep and filled with an honesty that contradicted the lie he was pushing. "I was a surgeon. I was at the top of my game. Fast-tracking it to become chief of surgery. After the accident, I lost it all. I have a faint tremor in my hand that will not ever heal and be steady enough for me to perform surgery. So this…career change would give me a chance to reclaim some of what I've lost."

"I'm sorry," she whispered, feeling the sting of tears. She blinked rapidly, trying to rein in the emotion that was making it hard for her to breathe. She had cost this man his career? There wasn't a day that went by that she didn't remember that accident. The burning smell of exhaust and oil still haunted her dreams at night, and the sound of that man's cry mingled with her son's still had the power to stop her heart. Sometimes she relived that day as a reminder of all the things she had to be grateful for. And sometimes she relived that day as a reminder of what she'd come so close to losing.

Maybe this could be her way of repaying him, if only a little. She was indebted to him. How could she say no to the man who had saved the most precious person in the world to her? Guilt swam through her, threatening to drown her. But she couldn't afford to sink. She needed to be strong. If she knew exactly what he needed of her, then she could make a To-Do list and everything would be okay…

She drew a shaky breath. "Exactly what do you need me to do again?"

He broke out into a smile that had the same effect as clouds parting on an overcast day to let the most glorious light in. Evan Manning was gorgeous. "You can start work on Monday. I'll just go over your résumé, make a few calls for references, and we'll be good to go."

She nodded. She owed him. She would do this for him. "I've worked in doctor's offices since high school, and always in the city. This could be a nice change."

He nodded. "Good, good."

There was just one thing she needed a little more clarification on. She leaned forward. "Can you give me a few more details about the fiancée thing?"

"Right. Just a few events. I'll be having a meeting here with the director, and he said he wants to meet my family— which would be you. Oh, and I guess you could attend this crazy person's wedding I have to go to. That way my family will meet you, and that'll get them off our backs. Then there's a huge hospital gala in Toronto," he said walking back to his desk.

Grace stood in the middle of the room, feeling as though she were on some alien vessel ready to fly off to Planet Crazy. Galas and weddings? The last event she went to was the kindergarten spring concert. And even there she'd felt out of place. She would disappoint him. She didn't move in his circles. *She was wearing a freaking Spider-Man shoelace in her hair.*

"Dr. Manning, I don't know I could pull that off."

He walked back over to her, standing close, and she tilted her head back slightly to meet his blue eyes. She didn't know if she was comforted by the knowledge or not, but his expression wasn't laced with even a hint of insanity or doubt. "You can. I'll take the lead. Just follow along and pretend we're in love."

His deep voice was filled with confidence, his gaze unwavering. She crossed her arms and ignored the flush that was making its way up her neck at the mention of them being in love. "I'm not a great liar—"

"This isn't a lie that will hurt anyone. Most likely no one at the gala will even speak to you. And you don't have to lie to my family."

She frowned, thinking. She would be helping out the man who had saved their lives; she would get a steady job. After the accident, she'd had to quit full-time work because Christopher had needed so much care. He'd been in the hospital for a month. Financially, she'd barely been holding on before, and after, she'd resorted to cutting so many corners, it had felt like they'd previously been living in luxury. She'd never forget the night Chris was discharged from the hospital, and instead of taking him home to his own bed, they had been greeted by a lock on their front door. She'd been a few weeks behind on rent and the landlord had locked them out. The next morning she'd begged him and they'd regained access by Grace withdrawing money from her credit cards to pay rent. The rest of the year all she'd been able to manage was part-time work, but then they'd let her go last week. She couldn't keep living so close to the edge. Not with Christopher. Today's job interview in Toronto was for a full-time position. But what Evan was offering...

"It's one month. Then I'll be back in Toronto, and Dr. Chalmers will be here. He's great to work for. And there's an impressive benefits package. I also know a nice house I can get for you and your son for a few months. It's on the river. It's been newly renovated and restored. It's even fully furnished, because the house is staged for sale."

She broke his stare and looked down at her shoes. She was torn between embarrassment and elation. A furnished house on the river? Full benefits? "That doesn't really sound like something I could afford—"

"I know the owners. You tell me what you can pay, and I'll see to the rest."

Her heart pounded. This was too good to be true. "What about school for my son?"

"Great elementary school in town. My niece goes there. She's about his age. I'm sure you can get him in there next week. People in Red River are really accommodating, friendly. If they can't take him on Monday, you can bring him with you to work."

This was absurd…and compelling. It would mean doing something impulsive. But it would also mean a steady income, a place to live, and a new start. After the year they'd had, maybe this was just what they needed. "Well, I need to see the school. I can't just stick him in any old place. It's not that he even liked his other school, really—"

"Go today. I'm sure they'll give you a tour. Oh and uh," he cleared his throat, his blue eyes doing a rapid perusal of her from head to toe, "you need to dress for the job."

She glanced down at her clothes and tried not to look embarrassed. She hadn't exactly dressed to impress. And it was pretty obvious she was so not the woman a man like Evan Manning would date, let alone be engaged to. "I used to wear scrubs at the other office."

"Not here. Just business casual. Fridays are usually even more casual."

*Business casual.* The closest she had to that was *broke-mom casual,* and that would not do. But she also didn't have the spare cash lying around to invest in a new wardrobe.

"I also need you to dress for your job as my fiancée."

Her mortification peaked to an all-time high, and she

couldn't help but pat her hair gently. Maybe at one time she'd have been insulted, but she knew she wasn't the type of woman Dr. Manning would date, and there was no point in being egotistical about it. "How exactly would your fiancée dress?"

He gave her a dispassionate once-over, and she fought the urge to cross her arms defensively. Again, this didn't matter. This was not a personal thing. Obviously the man could attract anyone he wanted, so it would be unbelievable for him to have a frumpy, ho-hum fiancée. "Feminine. Stylish. Sophisticated."

Those were three adjectives that could in no way describe any of the clothes in her small closet at the moment. Really, what did she wear? When she had her medical-receptionist job, most of the girls wore scrubs, which had been great for her, because she could buy them super cheap. But what he was asking she did not have the budget for. Her cheeks warmed like her old toaster oven about to overheat. They were not in the same league at all.

"I'm not really sure I have the clothes—"

"Then we'll go shopping." He tilted his watch toward him. "How about tomorrow afternoon?"

She opened her mouth, but the words were stuck.

"I'll pay of course."

"This seems really sudden. I mean, I don't even know you—"

"You don't have to. We're not going to be living together. This is just for appearances. One or two social events—in public—and the secretarial position. This should be easy and mutually beneficial. Don't make this into a bigger deal—"

"Uh, it is a big deal. I'm going to uproot my life and my

child's life and pretend that I'm your wife. I don't even know anything about you or your family—"

"No problem. You'll meet them. They hover like harmless, overzealous vultures. And then a couple weeks from now we have to go to this crazy lady's wedding. I think you'd really like my family. For some reason, they have tons of friends."

She broke his intense blue stare and looked down at her feet. Sensible running shoes. Cheap running shoes. Not the shoes this man's future wife would wear. Panic and adrenaline began pumping through her veins. This was nuts. But if she said no and walked out of here, what was she going back to Toronto for? No job, crappy apartment, no friends… but how would she pull off being his wife?

"Hey, Grace, it's not like we're actually going to have to get married at the end of this. We're not hurting anyone." He darted a glance at Chris. "This might be a really good opportunity for you to put away some extra money for your son. To get ahead. A little something for yourself, too."

She sighed. It would mean free expenses for a month. And a salaried position again. "I pay rent in Toronto—"

"I'll cover it. I'll pay your last month's rent and any fee for breaking your lease, and you can give your landlord notice. That will give you time to slowly get your things on the weekends. No rush or stress. Plus a whole new wardrobe. Expenses at the rental house will be covered as well for at least a few months. And this job has a great salary. Think of this as a new start. Plus you'll be living in a town that's great for raising a family."

"I don't do spontaneous things. I like lists and making plans weeks in advance. I just need some time—"

"I'm afraid that's the only thing I can't give you. The receptionist walked out of here today leaving me with no one. I'm here helping out an old friend, and I can't tell him that after a week I've lost his secretary."

And here was the saint side of him again—he had put his career on hold to fill in for a doctor? He had saved her and Chris from a burning car, and now he was offering her a deal she just couldn't refuse. This one man, this virtual stranger was doing more for her than Christopher's father ever had. She squeezed her eyes shut. She owed him.

"Just pack up the essentials. Whatever you need you can get next weekend. I'll have your place ready for you tomorrow." He pulled out a notepad and scribbled out an address and handed it to her. "Here. Go to this address tomorrow morning at nine. Then we can go shopping after. You can spend all day settling in on Sunday. And you'll be all set for Monday."

She drew a deep breath. This was the craziest thing she'd ever contemplated. But what did she have to lose? The apartment she struggled to pay rent for in Toronto wasn't anything to feel proud about. She didn't exactly live in the nicest area of the city, and she wasn't pleased with Chris's school. Her neighborhood was nothing like this charming little town. Maybe this was a chance for a new beginning. Something positive. "My only other question is about my son," she said, lowering her voice. "I don't want him thinking we are really going to get married. I don't want him getting attached to you or thinking you'll be his father."

He didn't say anything, so she pressed on. "Dr. Manning, I don't want him getting his hopes up that he'll have a father in his life."

Something flickered in his expression, and his mouth softened. "Of course." His deep voice held a note of compassion, and the man she had already thought handsome had now become the hero she'd imagined.

She forced a smile and extended her hand. "Okay, my only stipulation is that if I'm not happy with the school or the house, I can back out of this deal. Or if I feel this isn't working out for Christopher, I can walk."

"Deal. But somehow, I think this town is going to grow on you. And this will be the best gamble you've ever taken." He smiled, and her stomach dropped and fluttered in a way that made her aware of Evan Manning in every possible way.

His large, warm hand enveloped hers, and she had the distinct impression that she was getting into far more than he'd stated.

# Chapter Three

Evan stared in disgust as an enormous, oval-shaped platter of fried bacon, eggs, and home fries was placed in front of him. He looked up at his two brothers, who had already eagerly begun devouring the heart-attack-on-a-plate in front of them.

"Are you guys kidding me?" he asked, leaning forward as a piece of bacon virtually disappeared into Quinn's mouth.

"What?" Jake asked before taking a gulp of coffee.

"How often do you two eat here?" He frowned, glancing at the toast. Maybe he could eat that. Then he looked at the amount of butter that was dripping down and thought twice. He reached for his coffee.

"Every Monday at six a.m. You know that—we've been trying to get you to join us for years," his eldest brother, Quinn, answered, shoving some home fries down his throat.

"You're lucky we made this exception for you and are meeting on a Friday," Jake said, with a mouthful of bacon.

Evan stared at the two of them. They were both in their thirties and in great shape. But if this was the way they ate...

"When was the last time you guys had your cholesterol checked? Physicals?"

Jake and Quinn exchanged a look. He knew that look all too well. No one was taking the kid brother seriously, regardless of the "Doctor" that preceded his name. There was nothing more humbling than hanging around his brothers. The only time they'd cut him any slack was after the accident. But he couldn't handle their pitying looks, so had quickly made it clear that he didn't accept their sympathy. It had been way too uncomfortable.

Jake leaned forward. "You're not giving me a physical."

Evan scowled at him. "I wasn't offering. I was thinking of referring you to the vet."

"There's nothing wrong with either of us," Quinn said.

"Yeah, we burn it all off. You should stop being such a tight-ass and loosen up," Jake said.

"I'm not being a tight-ass. Do you have any idea how many heart attacks I've seen?"

Jake's groan stopped him from continuing. "Lighten up, Ev. Seriously, this is why you don't have a woman in your life. Do you order salad for dinner when you take a woman out? A woman doesn't like a man who eats less than her." His brother stabbed a forkful of egg in the air.

Evan resisted the urge to chuck his coffee onto Jake's lap. He looked down at his plate and poked a piece of the egg. "I don't eat salads for dinner, and I do have a woman in my life. Not that it's any of your business."

Quinn smiled. "Nice. Who? Natalia? Holly kept telling me she thought that Nat had a thing for you."

Jake snorted. "Are you kidding? He can't go out with a baker. He'll be telling her not to use too much butter or sugar."

"Not Nat."

Quinn leaned forward. "Then who?"

Evan leaned back in the booth and stretched slowly, enjoying making his brothers wait.

"Spill it," Jake growled.

"Her name is Grace." He took a sip of coffee and checked his BlackBerry just to piss them off a little more.

Jake yanked his phone out of his hand. "And?"

"She's the woman I need the coach house for." That was about all he wanted to spill about Grace. Because, hell, Grace had taken him by surprise yesterday. Last night, instead of sleeping, he'd found himself thinking about her. And how she was going to be his pretend wife. And receptionist. And that she was the woman he'd pulled from the car. And her kid. He'd remember the feel of his arms around his neck for the rest of his life…long after this stint in Red River was over.

Quinn slid a keychain and keys across the table, and Evan slipped them in his pocket, grateful for the distraction. "Thanks, I appreciate you guys helping me out."

Jake slowly placed his mug down on the table. "You're using the vacant coach house, on the property we just restored and have up for sale, to shack up a woman?"

"Relax. It's a business arrangement. And turns out she's not some random woman."

"Oh, good. I was just thinking that you were so desperate because you managed to lose Chalmers's long-time receptionist after only a week and now had to resort to offering room and board for new employees."

Evan clenched his teeth as he forced a casual smile. It was a lot harder to accomplish than he thought. But he had no choice. Every time he engaged in conversation with Jake, he found himself unable to fully let his brother have it. He stopped short. Because of what Jake had revealed to them. The truth about their father had hit him hard. Jake's entire life had been a lie, and the resentment he'd felt toward his brother growing up now made him feel like an ass.

"So how'd you find someone new so fast?" Quinn asked.

"You remember the woman and kid I saved in that car accident?"

Jake motioned to the waiter for more coffee and then turned back to Evan. "Uh, not really, since you never talk about it."

Fair enough. He'd always shut down a conversation when it turned to the accident. He didn't enjoy talking about his feelings to anyone. And ever since his brothers had gotten married, they actually engaged in those types of conversations every now and then.

"Well, her."

Silence. John, the waiter and owner, poured their cups and then quickly left the table, in a hurry to help the other patrons in the busy restaurant.

Jake eyed Quinn and then leaned forward. "Okay, this is painful to listen to, Ev. You have to hurry up and spill the details. I'm the brother in this family who doesn't talk. Not you. So explain."

"All right. Well apparently she'd been trying to get in touch with me this last year—"

"Why didn't you ever go see her?"

He balled up his napkin and then dropped it onto his plate. "I needed to move on from what happened. I didn't want to know who they were. Hell, I didn't want to see anyone for a long time, least of all them. It would drag me back to that day, and I didn't want to think of everything I'd lost."

Silence, and then his ever-sensible eldest brother spoke up. "Evan, you saved a woman's life. And her son's. I know you had to pay the price with the damage to your hand and then losing that Alexandra woman. Maybe this is a good reason for you to stick around and settle in Red River. Like it or not, buddy, this is your town."

Evan stared at Quinn for a moment before looking down. He didn't want to be talking about any of this. Especially his hand. As for Alex, the fellow surgeon who ditched him, he was over it. Or her. He suspected his family was hoping that this brief stint in Red River would mean he'd come back here for good. But that was the last thing he wanted. Filling in for Dr. Chalmers had been enlightening, and he knew there was no way he'd ever be satisfied with family practice. There was no thrill, no adrenaline rush. Despite not being able to perform surgery, he still preferred the inside of the ER to that tiny office.

He hadn't been ready for his career to be ripped away from him. There was no way either of his brothers could understand—they were both family men. He wasn't made like them—his feelings didn't run as deep. No one had ever come close to meaning more to him than his job. So how could he tell them that he wanted to get the hell away from this town, first chance he got?

He cleared his throat and forced a smug expression on

his face. "What is this? What is wrong with you two? We used to talk about game scores and work. All this personal crap is getting a little much, especially without any beer around. You both need to get your estrogen levels checked," he said, pleased with himself when they both gagged on their bacon.

"Yeah, funny. When are you going back to the ER again?" Jake asked with a smirk.

"So here's the thing, I'm not going back to the ER."

Quinn smiled. "Red River finally won you over? What was it? Being back with us? The kids?"

He swallowed his coffee alongside a large dose of guilt at his brother's question. "Not exactly. I'm in the running for a position as chief director for a new group of medical clinics."

"That's great. Where are the clinics? Toronto?"

Evan nodded.

"You never mentioned this before, right?"

He shook his head. "It's something that just fell into my lap. I was recommended for the position by the chief of staff at the hospital and met with the board of Medcorp."

Quinn frowned. "Medcorp? Aren't they private plastic-surgery clinics?"

Evan nodded.

"You're going to work in a plastic-surgery clinic?"

His fingers tightened around the handle of the cup. "I'm going to run the clinics. CEO to be exact."

Neither of them said anything for a minute. Then Quinn piped up. "Well how's that exciting? I mean, you still won't be a surgeon. And you won't be in the ER. So how's being a director of a bunch of private clinics thrilling?"

Money. Power. Prestige. That was it in a nutshell.

Jake placed his fork down and gave him a classic no-bullshit face. "So you're going from saving people's lives to dealing with boob jobs and lipo? That's better than family practice?"

He knew they wouldn't get it. He didn't bust his ass, graduate from high school and university early, didn't push to be the best only to end up in Red River making chitchat with the townies. No freaking way was he settling for this. "How is Holly feeling?" Evan asked, trying to divert the attention off of him. Quinn was very predictable: all Evan needed to do was ask the man something about his pregnant wife, and that would be it.

Quinn's face softened at the mention of his wife. Worked like a charm every time. "Good. Counting down the days till the baby is due. Her OB is going on vacation, so she's worried about that, even though there is someone filling in for her. And she's driving herself—and me—nuts trying to organize everything. Every minor detail. The nursery has been set up for three months already. Now she's worried that she's washed all the baby clothes too early and needs to wash them again," he said with a laugh.

"Yeah, that phase almost killed me when Claire went through it," Jake said, taking a sip of coffee.

Evan ducked his head. His brothers were talking about nesting and babies. And they were acting as though this were a normal occurrence. How times had changed. "Well, tell Holly if she needs anything or isn't feeling well, to come and see me."

Quinn's eyes narrowed. "I think you can stop with the offers for family physicals. She doesn't need to see you, Ev."

Evan rolled his eyes. At least that sounded more like his

brother. "Look, man, I have no intention of going anywhere near where you've been, so relax."

Jake cleared his throat. "So back to the woman situation—"

"There's no situation. I better get moving. I need to get a jog in, especially after eating this trash," Evan grumbled, rising.

"Uh, so when are we going to meet this woman? Not that I really care or anything," Jake said shifting his eyes guiltily. "But Claire will kill me if I don't get details."

"The wedding is soon enough. Don't show up at the office this week."

"You wish. You're bringing her to Eunice's wedding?"

Evan shrugged, trying to put Eunice Jacobs's garlicky toe out of his mind. "Well, I thought that way Grace could meet all of you at once and get it over with, so you don't have to spy on me around town and then blame it on your wives."

Jake snorted. "Yeah, like we'd ever do that."

"Hey, you're still coming for dinner Sunday night, right? Holly has some crazy idea that this will be the last Sunday night dinner before she goes into labor. And Ella keeps talking about how you promised to lend her your stethoscope for some doll examination," Quinn said with a chuckle. Evan smiled in return. His niece was adorable. And totally smart. She and his nephew were the only kids he liked being around.

"Absolutely wouldn't miss it. Apparently, there's a flu going around her doll community, so we're opening up a hospital in her room," Evan said, pulling out his wallet.

"Well, you have fun playing with dollies Sunday night,

Ev," Jake said with a smug smile.

"You bet," he said throwing down a ten-dollar bill. "But Ella already told me that Uncle Jake plays dollies the best. Something about your high-pitched voice." Quinn's deep laughter and Jake's expletives followed him out into the warm, fresh air.

Nothing like time with his brothers to bring him back to his roots. No one in the world could drive him crazier than his family.

# Chapter Four

"Chris, don't go too close to the water!" Grace yelled as her son scooped up a handful of rocks at the river's edge. Christopher, she'd discovered, could throw rocks into any body of water for hours at a time. She glanced down at her watch. They still had an hour before it was time to meet Dr. Manning at their "new house." She hadn't known what traffic would be like, taking the long, spineless-person route again. Turned out, the country roads had been quiet, and they'd gotten here from Toronto much faster than she'd predicted.

As soon as they had left his office yesterday, she and Christopher had walked the small Red River downtown area. She had been in a slight daze, but after seeing the small school and meeting the principal and the kindergarten teacher, she'd been much more excited. Christopher was thrilled with the school and the large playground. The town was totally charming, like right off the front of a postcard.

She had tried to be as honest as possible with Christopher

and told him if they loved it in Red River, then they'd live here. But for now, they were helping out Dr. Manning, and it was a nice thing to do considering. Chris seemed to love that idea that they were coming to Evan's rescue. She let him enjoy that feeling. The last thing she wanted was for him to feel guilty. But guilt had followed *her* all the way back to Toronto yesterday. She had cost Evan his career as a surgeon.

Once they were back in their apartment, she'd spent the night after Chris went to bed making a To-Do list that went on for pages and then packing up their things. She was upset that there wasn't enough room in her small car to take even a few of her painting supplies. Well, that would be for next weekend. Or whenever she got her first paycheck and they could splurge on the tank of gas it would take them to get there and back.

Of course, on this morning's drive, her nerves had set in. She had never done anything this impulsive. She'd always lived in Toronto. In an apartment and, at one time, a shelter. And after her mother had died, in a city of millions, she'd felt so alone. She'd lost touch with the few high school friends she'd had. She'd always had a part-time job in school, because she wanted to help her mom with bills. She never really had time to pursue other friendships. Then after that she'd met Brian and thought she'd met a truly dependable man. A man who would stand by his wife and child, a man nothing like her father…and she couldn't have been more wrong.

Well, she'd never make that mistake again. She was fully content being a single mother. She would never let another man come close to destroying her. And then, in fifteen years, when Chris was an adult, she intended to adopt five cats, gain fifty pounds, and never use antifrizz products on her hair again.

"Don't worry, Mom!" Christopher yelled, wobbling slightly as he shot her a toothy grin before chucking a rock into the water. The resounding gulp from the river as it swallowed the rock earned a loud, "*Yessss*." She sat down on one of the large boulders, took a sip of her coffee from the paper cup, and watched. The river was clear and running smoothly, filled with the abundant spring rain. The trail system along the river ran for miles according to the signs, the gravel path winding by the banks of the water. Green grass and meticulously landscaped gardens made the park a gorgeous place to sit on a spring day.

A pretty, albeit very pregnant woman, walking with a little girl along the trail appeared. The little girl approached Christopher, and he handed her a fistful of rocks. The two of them were soon completely preoccupied with seeing who could make the biggest splash.

Grace rose and walked over to the where the woman was standing.

"They seem to have made friends," the woman said, smiling as Grace approached. She extended her hand. "I'm Holly, and that's my daughter, Ella."

"Hi, I'm Grace. Nice to meet you. That's my son Christopher," she said smiling. This was small-town life. People actually just struck up conversations with strangers. She looked over at Christopher, who was chattering a mile a minute with the little girl. The woman didn't even look her up and down or make her feel awkward for not being dressed fashionably. It was strange; in the city, no one cared to know more about her. There were rich people, normal people, and homeless people. They all walked sided by side on the streets, and she just blended in as one of them. Here, everyone would soon figure out what their situation was really like. It was disconcerting. She hoped that the kids at Christopher's school were kind...

"Do you mind if we sit down and watch? I really need to get off my feet," Holly said with a laugh. Grace gave her a sympathetic smile and nodded, walking over to the nearby bench.

"When are you due?" she asked once they'd seated.

"Not soon enough. Another six weeks, but right about now it feels like I'll be pregnant forever," she said with a groan.

"I remember that feeling," Grace said, taking a sip of coffee. She would never forget the end of her pregnancy. It had been horrible, those last few weeks. She'd never felt so alone or so scared. First her mother—the dearest person in the world to her—had died, and then her world and her stability had been ripped apart when Christopher's father just walked out on them without warning, without leaving a dime, without leaving a phone number. Somehow, she had found the strength to go on. But there were nights, lying awake in her dark room, that the ache for her mother would fill her until she was forced to release the tears that she controlled on a daily basis. She had no one to rely on; no one had her back anymore. It had been a crash course in reality, and she'd learned the hard way to never let her and her son be vulnerable to anyone else again.

"I shouldn't complain; it's been a pretty good pregnancy, and my husband's been wonderful. I guess I'm just anxious at this point." She took a deep breath and turned, smiling at

Grace. Her green eyes lit up. "Enough about me though. Are you new to Red River?"

Grace tilted her head. "Sort of. I just accepted a job as a receptionist for a doctor's office."

"That's great. I hope you like it."

Grace tucked a strand of hair behind her ears. "Me, too. It's a big change for us. But I'm starting to think we'll like small-town life."

"Red River is one of the nicest places in the area to raise a family."

She crossed her legs, taking a sip of coffee. "So you grew up here?"

Holly nodded. "I went away to school and worked in Toronto as an interior designer for a while before relocating back to Red River. I never thought I'd move back here, but destiny sort of had other plans for me, and I married the man of my dreams, and well, the rest is history," she said with a smile that held such undiluted happiness that Grace couldn't even imagine.

Christopher gave Grace joy, and there wasn't anyone in the world more important to her, but the choices she'd made and the regrets she had kept her from feeling true happiness. She noticed the way Holly looked at her daughter, the peace on her face. The sparkling ring on her finger, a symbol that she was still with the father of her child.

"That's wonderful," Grace said after a few seconds of silence. "Red River is a pretty little town."

"It is. Where are you from?"

"Toronto."

"Oh wow! So you're a city girl, too. This might take some getting used to at first, but it's a great place for kids, a real sense of community. Let me know if you need anything at all. Information about the school, whatever. And look at your son and my daughter—they get along so well."

"I'm planning on enrolling Chris at Red River Elementary. He's so excited about it."

"Oh nice. I bet they'll be in the same class. There's only one class per grade," she said with a laugh.

Grace blinked. "Wow, what a change from what we're used to."

"I know. So how long have you been a receptionist?"

Grace liked everything about this woman. She was positive, friendly, and someone she would have loved to be friends with. She hadn't had a true friend in years. She couldn't remember the last time she'd just sat and chatted with another woman. She'd become closed off and so busy trying to do everything that her social life was nonexistent. And going out would have meant hiring a sitter, which would have meant spending money.

But sitting next to Holly made her reflect on everything she was lacking. She was embarrassed. Embarrassed that they had nothing. Embarrassed by having a job that wasn't her real passion, that didn't sum up who she was. It still hurt, admitting that she hadn't pursued her dream of being an artist. It always felt like a cop-out. She couldn't cut it, so she had given up. She didn't drive on highways anymore. She let fear dominate so many areas of her life.

"Ever since high school, really. My mother worked in a doctor's office. Single mom. To help make some extra money, I'd go in with her after school and do filing. And then after that, I got a full-time job while pursuing art school in the evenings. Christopher was unexpected. I had to take a bit of a break from it. I just ran out of time, between work and raising him. Maybe this year," she said, quickly trying to smile so that it didn't sound so pathetic.

"Don't be hard on yourself," Holly said softly. Grace swallowed hard, as she saw the compassion in her new friend's eyes. "I remember the first few months here with Ella, and I was by myself trying to raise her. I know it's hard, all on your own. You can do it. You just need time and support," she said. Her eyes lit up a second later. "Do you still have all your work? A portfolio?"

Grace nodded slowly, toying with the lid of her cup. She was curious as to why Holly had been all on her own. Unless Ella wasn't her husband's child. She wasn't about to pry and act nosy. Besides, the woman was asking about Grace's portfolio. What were the odds of meeting someone who actually cared enough to ask about her art?

"Our family construction and renovation company just finished a project, for a new art gallery. I did all the interior design work. It would be perfect. They're over in Port Ryan, and that entire area is filled with artisan boutiques, studios, wineries, even a little live theater. I could talk to them—I would love to tell them about you. Maybe they'll want to see your work. Small areas like this love supporting local artists."

Grace sucked in a breath. Seriously? She felt tears sting the back of her eyes at the unbridled generosity from a person she only just met. She wanted to be able to convey her gratitude without looking desperate. When was the last time she'd met anyone willing to do anything for her? What if Holly saw her work and hated it? What if the gallery said no? She'd lost her confidence. She had been fighting for years to get her work placed. And now…

"At least let me try," her friend said gently, as though she sensed Grace's hesitation.

Grace thought of Christopher, of their apartment back in the city. And then she thought how it would feel to one day be a paid artist, to tell her son that she'd followed her dreams. And he could, too. She needed to get herself together and stop acting like a ninny without a backbone. She was tougher than this.

She nodded a second later. "I'd really appreciate that, Holly. I just…maybe I can take a few days to think about it." More like a few days to get the courage to put her work out there. She needed to be strong enough to deal with the crushing disappointment that would come if the gallery rejected her outright.

Holly did a semiflail. "Sure. I think this will be great. So what's the office in Red River that you're starting work at?"

Grace took a deep breath, ready to tell her, when Holly interrupted, her eyes on the trail. "Oh, look, it's my brother-in-law. I'll introduce you; he's a doctor. My husband's brother is a total catch—and he's single."

Grace looked over, not able to stand, shock anchoring her butt to the bench as Evan Manning slowed his jog to pick up Ella and swing her around. Holly was already walking over to Evan. Evan Manning was her only friend's brother-in-law.

Grace walked as slowly as she could without looking obvious. She was very aware that Evan's eyes were on hers. Evan was still breathing deeply from his run, and she allowed herself to really look at him, her eyes safely hidden behind her sunglasses. He wiped his brow with the edge of his blue, long-sleeved shirt, revealing a perfectly flat, sculpted set of abs. He was long and lean, broad shoulders and ripped… *Snap out of it, Grace.* He was her employer. He had no interest in her whatsoever. Which was totally fine. Because she wouldn't know what to do with a man like Evan.

Her heart skipped a beat as Evan leaned down and ruffled Christopher's hair while holding his niece. "Ella, you're getting so tall, I can barely pick you up anymore," he joked, pretending to drop her. His well-defined biceps were a clear indication that was not accurate at all. Ella squealed, and he placed her on the ground.

"Hi, Grace," Evan said with a smile. "I, uh, see you've met," he said to Holly and Grace.

"We just met," Holly said. "I didn't know *you* two knew each other."

"Grace came in to the office yesterday with Christopher, and she accepted the position as receptionist for Chalmers."

Holly was looking back and forth between them. "How *wonderful*."

"I think it'll work out great for both of us."

Grace felt her body spark to life at the sight of that smile. Wide smile, perfect white teeth in a bronzed face. And he had the clearest blue eyes she'd ever seen. And he hadn't shaved this morning. He was slightly scruffy. A complete contrast to the polished look from yesterday but equally delicious. She needed to get it together. There would never be anything between her and the hot doctor who dated *feminine, stylish, sophisticated* women. She needed to remember that, working for him this month. She needed to remember for her own sake, and for Christopher's.

• • •

*Dammit, this town was too small. And filled with too many of his family members.* Evan stared at Grace, actually finding himself without words. Her hair was disheveled but shiny and full of gorgeous, slightly wild curls that were insanely appealing. She was still wearing the frumpy clothes. But she was gorgeous.

"What a small world this is," Holly said looking between them. Evan groaned inwardly. He could already see the machinations forming in his sister-in-law's mind. Holly and Claire had made finding him a woman a top priority. Like he was a damn charity case.

"Well, more like small town," Evan answered, his eyes on Grace. Her sunglasses were off, and she was watching the kids, who were by the water again.

"I can't believe how lucky I am," she said. "Dr. Manning—"

"Evan," he corrected.

Her smiled wobbled slightly. "Evan here, um, offered me a job and a place to live—"

Holly clutched Grace's arm. "*You're* going to live in the coach house?"

Evan stifled his groan. Holly looked like she was about to go into premature labor with that bit of news.

Grace was nodding.

"I decorated that house. Oh, I hope you like it."

"I'm sure we will—Chris, what are you doing?" Grace called out. Evan tore his eyes away from hers and followed her gaze. He tried not to laugh out loud as her son and his niece attempted to push a small boulder into the river.

"Ella, be careful!" Holly called out.

"Mom, we need to get this rock into the water," Christopher said, putting his hands on his hips.

"No, you don't," Grace countered. "There are plenty of small stones—"

"We need to make a gigantic splash!" Ella yelled.

"You know, there is something to be said for a making a splash," Evan said turning to them. Christopher turned to look up at Evan, his face lit with something that made Evan's smile waver. Something in that little boy's expression hit him in the gut.

"See, Dr. Nevan knows!"

"Evan," Ella corrected with a shake of her head.

"How about I help them get this thing into the water?" Evan asked, feeling inexplicably happy that the kids were now laughing and jumping up and down, clearly anticipating their victory. He would do anything for his niece and his nephew. It was odd; he'd never really been the kid type, but being around Ella and Michael always put him in a good mood. And he had to admit this Christopher kid was a bit of a character.

"*Yes!* Uncle Evan is the best!"

Grace smiled, and Evan decided he needed to focus on the kids and not how full and tempting Grace's lips were. Or why her smile affected him like that. Or why he wasn't noticing the boring clothes she was wearing. Maybe it was because she was one of the few women he knew who was just naturally beautiful.

"Just this one, okay, Ella? We have to get home after this," Holly said.

Both kids nodded.

"Dr. Nevan, look at these worms," Christopher said, pointing at squirming creatures they'd just uncovered. Evan tried his best to answer the barrage of questions about slime as best he could, drawing on some of his own childhood memories of worms.

"Mom, come see all these worms! Can we take one home?"

"No, you should probably let the worms stay where they are. I don't think we should be bringing worms into a new house. You give the worms one last look and then get moving that rock okay?" Grace said, her voice warm and patient. Evan liked the way she handled Christopher, noticing the way her features softened whenever she looked at her son.

"Okay, guys, let's get this thing into the water. Ready? One, two, three," Evan yelled, and pushed the small boulder off the wall of rocks and into the river with a massive splash. Christopher and Ella's exuberant jumping and cheering made him smile.

"Dr. Nevan, you're the best. You're so strong. Do you think you're stronger than Batman?"

Evan stifled his laugh.

"No of course not. But my dad is," Ella said proudly. "And then maybe Uncle Evan is tied with Uncle Jake. No wait," she said, tapping her chin. "Maybe Uncle Evan *is* a superhero. You know what he did—"

"Nothing, I did nothing. I'm not a superhero, but thanks, sweetie," he said, cutting off his niece. He knew exactly what she was about to say. "Is Batman your favorite, Christopher?"

Christopher nodded rapidly. "But sometimes I like Spider-Man, because I really like spiders."

Evan nodded, rubbing his chin. "Yeah, that's a good point. I like spiders, too," he said. "But I think it's okay to keep changing which superhero is your favorite." Christopher kind of reminded him of himself when he was a kid.

"Hey, Mom, you know what this reminds me of?"

Evan turned to look at Grace whose smiled dipped slightly. She shook her head.

"It reminds me of that night I came home from the hospital—"

"No, Chris, it does *not*—"

Christopher perched his hands on his hips. "Yes, yes, it does! It's exactly—"

"Christopher, stop—"

"When our apartment door had a lock on it and we couldn't get in so—"

The gorgeous color in Grace's face had vanished, leaving her white. She was shaking her head, but her kid wasn't getting it. Evan's stomach churned uncomfortably at where this story was going.

"My mom said we could go to the park and then camp out in our car! Isn't that cool? So we went down to the water before it was time to sleep and threw rocks and then this crazy bad guy—"

"Christopher, that's a private—"

Ella poked Christopher's shoulder. "Wow a real bad guy?"

He gave her a serious nod and then continued, "And Mom said if he didn't leave us alone, she was going to—"

"Stop it. Stop talking," Grace snapped. An uncomfortable silence hung between all of them, holding them there while Christopher frowned at his mother. Evan hated all the missing pieces to this story. He hated thinking of what the hell had happened. But right now, the humiliation that was etched so deeply in her face bothered him, and he wanted to help her.

"So, Grace I'll meet you at the house at nine? I just need to grab a quick shower, and I'll meet you there. And, uh..." He glanced over at Holly, who was standing at attention. Hopefully his sister-in-law would take the bait and the focus would be back on whatever it was she thought was going on between him and Grace and not on Christopher's story. "Then we'll do the shopping thing."

Holly lifted her sunglasses and eyed them both. "Shopping?"

Perfect. Grace was nodding, but her face was still pale and she looked embarrassed. "We just need a few things and—"

"And I'm going to show them around the town. That's all," he said. The last thing he wanted was for Grace to feel awkward and rethink everything.

"That's great... I can't wait to see you again, Grace," Holly said smiling.

"Everything okay, Holly?" Evan asked, noticing the way she was pressing her hand into her lower back.

"Hmm? Me, oh yeah, fine. Well, now that you mention it, I've been having horrid Braxton Hicks contractions for the past two weeks."

"You tell your OB?"

She nodded. "She said it was normal. I just hate to think I have six weeks of these ahead of me," she said with a groan.

"Well, just keep monitoring them. Take it easy. Get that brother of mine to do more. Put your feet up and relax a little when you get home," he said.

Holly nodded. "Thanks. Okay, Ella, we need to get going."

"See ya tomorrow, Chris," Ella said with a wave as she and Holly started the trail.

"See ya later, Ella! Bye," Christopher yelled.

"Wait! Holly?" Grace called.

Holly turned around.

"Um, yes. Definitely yes. I don't need more time to think about it. I'll take you up on your offer about the gallery."

Holly beamed at her, and Evan wondered what they were talking about. He shrugged it off. He'd witnessed Holly and Claire in action countless times, never really knowing what either of those two were up to.

"Great! I'll let you know as soon as I hear something." Holly gave a little wave as she and Ella made their way down the path. Grace turned to look up at him and flipped her sunglasses up onto her head, green eyes glittering with something that was familiar. Awareness.

"Mom, Dr. Nevan, look at this!" He tore his eyes away from hers to look over at Christopher. Evan felt something as he watched her son run toward them with at least a dozen worms squirming inside an empty coffee cup.

"Ugh, Chris, what is this? Isn't this my coffee cup?"

He gave his mom a sheepish grin, and Evan felt some of the tension leave his body. Her little boy was pretty hysterical. Evan glanced over at Grace who was shaking her head, a smile tugging at the corner of her lush mouth as she looked at her son.

"Look," he said shoving the cup at Evan. Evan held the cup for him while the little boy pleaded with his mother.

"We are not bringing these to a brand-new house," Grace said, with a laugh.

"What if I leave them in the backyard?"

Evan tilted the cup in Grace's direction. The kid's smiled widened, and he clasped his hands together like he was praying for a miracle. He totally knew how to work his mom. She let out a big sigh. "Fine. But nowhere near the back door." Evan handed him the cup, laughing.

"Yes!" Christopher yelled, jumping and almost chucking the contents of the cup at them.

Grace backed up a step, frowning as she watched him regain his balance.

"We really should get going, Chris," she said.

Evan tried to ignore the odd feeling that came over him when the little boy looked up at him. "But we're going to see you again soon, right?"

Evan cleared his throat. "Yeah. We'll probably be seeing a lot of each other."

"This is turning out to be the best day of my life!"

Evan didn't know whether that was the cutest thing he'd ever heard or the saddest. A feeling of dread trickled through him. He remembered Grace's words in the office yesterday, about Chris getting attached to him. The last thing he wanted was to mislead him. And yesterday, it had seemed impossible. But now, he was finding himself intrigued by them. He rolled his shoulders, attempting to regain some focus, some perspective. Instead, he just found himself wanting to know more about Grace.

# Chapter Five

"This place is so cool!"

"Stay there, Chris!" Grace yelled as her son bounded out of the car. He stopped and waved her over. Grace's insides liquefied as Evan stepped out of his shiny, black BMW. His dark hair was slightly rumpled, damp, and he was wearing a pair of low-slung cargoes that gave him a touch of badass that she never would have expected. His long-sleeve T-shirt was worn, stretching over his wide chest and loose around his middle. It had a University of Toronto logo on the front. His alma mater, no doubt. It reminded her that he was young for someone who'd accomplished so much. Which only made her feel more pathetic.

Her reaction to him was not promising for her productivity. She'd seen this man all of three times, and he looked completely different every time. This look…was a little too mouthwatering. He wasn't buttoned up and perfect. Well, he *was* perfect. He walked over to her car with the confidence of a man that knew his self-worth. Evan Manning was about as hot as a man could get. She was feeling so out of her element that a part of her just wanted to run, thank him for the position, and go back to their life in Toronto. But when she looked at her son, who was currently doing acrobatics around the massive front yard, she knew that would be impossible at this point.

"Dr. Nevan, this place is like a castle!"

She shut her eyes and placed her forehead down on the steering wheel with a sigh as Chris barreled into Evan. His deep voice carried across the open yard and she could hear the amusement in it as he spoke to her son. By the end of this, Evan Manning would have a very good idea of just how bad off they were. She was going to have a word with Christopher about appropriate topics to discuss in front of people. The way she'd snapped at Christopher made her feel like the worst mother—and then for it all to happen in front of Holly and Evan…

She needed to join them before Evan realized she was cowering in the car like a woman who hadn't been around a gorgeous guy in…how many years? She opened her eyes a moment later to take in the property. There was a large, New England-style home perched on a small hill with a winding drive. She knew that must have been the main house, and they were standing near the carriage house to the left of it. The grass was a vivid green, cut and kept beautifully. Dark green hedges lined the driveway and rows of oak trees and evergreens were scattered about the grounds. Sure beat an old apartment building in the wrong part of the city.

This house was a smaller version of the main one, with cedar shingles and pale blue siding. There were oversized iron coach lights beside the navy front door and two large, square urns filled with pansies. It was something she would have painted. The backdrop of the calm river made it almost too beautiful for her to enjoy it, knowing they would have to leave in a month or so.

Evan and Chris were standing on the front porch, peering into what used to be her coffee cup, no doubt discussing the worm situation.

*Get out of the car, Grace.* Maybe she'd cross off a few items from her To-Do list and then go. Yes, that would calm her down, give her some control back. She dragged out her notepad and orange crayon, smiling as her son yelled out, "Slime," and Evan's deep laugh carried across the yard and through her open car window.

After crossing off, "Meet Evan at new house," she added, "Buy new portfolio case for possible gallery interview."

"Making a grocery list?"

Grace yelped, orange crayon snapping in her hand as Evan's deep voice seemed to come out of nowhere. He was leaning against her car, arms splayed out on the hood as he watched her. He still hadn't shaved. She stared into his aviator glasses and checked her reflection to make sure she wasn't drooling. She needed to remember what he'd asked... She scrambled with her seat belt. "Yeah, but I'm good. All set."

He gave her a half smile that had full impact on her insides. "You should probably pick up that crayon so it doesn't melt all over your seat."

She nodded, tossing the crayon halves in her purse, and mentally added, "buy pens" to her list. He opened the door for her, and she tried to control the fluster as she walked beside him to the house.

He pointed beyond the house. "The back isn't fenced yet, but you don't have to worry about privacy. There's a second porch on the other side of the house with a swing."

"It's stunning," she said. She didn't know what else to say. She'd never lived in a house. She'd always lived in apartments. Or not even…

"Well, I hope you like the inside, too," Evan said as he held open the front door. Christopher disappeared through the door, and she stepped into the house. Evan's clean scent and aftershave teased her as she walked by him.

Her breath caught inside, anchored there by the feeling that this was too beautiful to be theirs. That if she let the breath out, all of this would blow away into nothing. This was just someone's guest home—for her and Chris, it was a dream house. Gleaming, dark hardwood floors spanned the open-concept main floor. A red-brick fireplace topped with a white mantle was the main focal point of the room, a flat-screen television mounted above. Two plush, ivory-colored sofas flanked the fireplace, and a tufted, red-and-white checked ottoman sat in between. The kitchen with custom white cabinets that soared to what must have been ten-foot ceilings beckoned, and the dark stone counters were honed to perfection. There was a breakfast bar with seating for four and a round white table with a vase of tulips in the middle. The backdrop of the water encompassed the entire rear wall, framed to perfection with the large patio doors.

She shook her head. "This is breathtaking, Dr.…*Evan*."

He shot her a smile. It was casual and to him must have meant nothing, as they did, but she felt it glide right through her body. How had this man come into their lives? "I'm glad you like it. Hey, Christopher, there are two bedrooms upstairs. You can take the smaller one and let your mom have the large one okay?"

Christopher jumped up and down. "Can I go up, Mommy?"

She nodded, forcing a smile as he grabbed his backpack and tore up the stairs.

"I can help you unload your car, and then we can get back into town for the shopping," he said already walking to the door.

Grace's feet were firmly planted to the ground, the definite feeling that this wasn't going to pan out holding them there. Nothing like this had ever happened to her.

It must be a mistake, and the sooner it was rectified, the better. The last thing she wanted was Christopher getting attached and then having to rip him away from this. This was a home that as much as she wished she could provide for her son, she could not. "Evan, there is no way the amount of money I told you we could pay for rent would cover a place like this."

He just smiled again, this time his expression softening. "Of course it can. My brothers are builders, and they restored the property—along with Holly, whom you just met. This house is vacant while it's up for sale, and they're not collecting any rent at all. Trust me, it's fine. There might be the odd showing, but you'll be given lots of notice. Nothing to worry about. You can stay here as long as the house is up for sale. And in Red River, a place like this might take a year to sell. You might as well enjoy it."

She crossed her arms in front of her and sighed. "Okay, well if they ever need us out sooner or anything, it's fine. We can find something else. I just don't want to take advantage

of their generosity. This is so much more than we need."

"Okay." He reached into his back pocket and pulled out an envelope. "Uh, here's a two-week advance—"

"Advance?" Grace stared at the envelope he held out.

He nodded, and she accepted it when he prompted again. His blue eyes were determined, the set of that jaw the same.

"You don't need—"

He shrugged. "I know. It's not a big deal."

This was awkward…and humiliating. She focused on the river over his shoulder. "It's because of what Christopher said. Listen you don't need to feel sorry for me; we're totally fine. That story was completely dramatized—"

"Grace, it's just an advance; it's not a gift. You're relocating. There are added expenses involved. Don't think twice about it."

She swallowed and crossed her arms. She couldn't turn that down, regardless of how embarrassed she was. "Thank you."

Something flickered across his eyes, but then he nodded. "You're welcome. Why don't you have a look upstairs, and I'll empty out your car for you?"

He was too much. Her gaze quickly darted to the large, bay window that overlooked the front yard. The towering oak trees and meticulous landscaping were perfect. Everything was perfect here. Except her crappy little car parked next to Evan's BMW. "Um, you know I don't mind going to the car."

"Grace, really it's fine. Have a look around the house, see what Christopher thinks, and I'll bring in your things. Then we can go shopping."

If there was a male fairy godmother, it would be him.

Although there wasn't really anything fairylike about the man. No, he was all lean lines and muscle. And there wasn't even anything really soft about the way he spoke to them. It was all in his casual actions, as though what he was doing was merely second nature. She had never been around a man like him. The memories she had of her father were vague, almost dreamlike, and there were no defining features or moments with him. Even Brian…they'd been so young, barely past their teens when they were together. And then he'd turned out to be such an incredible ass. Whatever redeeming qualities the man had went out the door when he did.

Evan Manning was every inch a man. The kind that a woman like her had no business fantasizing about.

"Mommy, you gotta come upstairs and see this! Two bathrooms up here!"

Of course, her son would be blown away by this. The entire upstairs was probably double the size of their apartment. And this was just the guesthouse for the main residence. But there was no reason to be mortified, because Evan wasn't even listening, his head bent as he scrolled through his phone. She looked up to see Christopher's head dangling over the railing. "I'm coming, Chris," she called up.

She walked up to Evan and extended her hand. "Um, here are my keys, but I can—"

"Thanks," he said absently, taking the keys from her.

His soft touch sent jolts of deep, powerful awareness through her. But only her, because he was already walking out the door while she was standing still like an idiot who'd never even been around a man—and trying not to check out his butt.

"Hurry up, Mommy. You gotta see your room!"

Grace climbed the stairs, shocked by how soft and plush the carpet felt beneath her feet. Tears pricked her eyes as she saw her son run across to a pale green bedroom with soaring ceilings and a massive window. She turned her head down the hall, slowly walking to the master bedroom. It was like something out of a magazine. This Holly woman had designed all of it? There was a fireplace and a huge, four-poster bed. All the furniture was dark, and the bright white duvet invited her to flop down and take a long, long nap. She was almost afraid to touch anything.

She walked over to the windows, holding her breath as she spotted Evan below. He was pulling bags out of their car. Most of their things were in plastic shopping bags, and she groaned out loud. What must he think of them? How different were they? Whoever these people were, the Mannings had welcomed them into this town like no one ever had. If only her mother were still here to share this with them.

• • •

Evan leaned against his car, waiting for Grace and Christopher to walk over to him once they were done parking their car. This entire situation was becoming slightly more complicated—and important. First off…Grace: she was gorgeous, in a completely accidental, not-even-trying-to-be kind of way. It was going to be difficult to ignore her, working with her day in and day out. There was something about her that went beyond the physical, because hell, hard as he tried, it was definitely impossible to check her out in the baggy clothes she wore. But there was a steely strength that he couldn't miss in those deep green eyes.

And then that made him think of what her kid had said about that night in the park in their car. And that made his gut clench. Just the thought of the two of them alone, in the city. And it made him want to find Chris's father and bash his face into a wall for not being around or giving them financial help. And hell if that wasn't problem number two: why did he care so much?

Their reactions to things—like the sense of wonder in Christopher's face at the house or the way he oohed and ahhed about Evan's car—assured him he'd made the right call by giving her that advance on her salary. Their clothes weren't expensive, and they were worn. Her car had been nothing but scrap metal, and when he'd taken out their belongings, most of them had been in shopping bags.

Grace was the complete opposite of the type of woman he was normally attracted to. First off, having a kid was like red-alert level for him to back off. Because women with kids would want things from him that he wasn't willing to give to anyone. And he was not father material.

The other thing about Grace that he'd never admit out loud was that he usually dated women who were more... accomplished. He liked to be challenged, intrigued...yet, there was something he caught in her eyes every now and then that made him wonder what her secrets were. There was a wisdom in her eyes that he couldn't ignore. Well, he was going to have to ignore it, because there was no way he could get involved with a woman with a child.

Evan pushed himself off from the side of the car as problem number three came barreling toward him at top speed: Christopher. This kid...he hadn't counted on how much he *wouldn't* be irritated by him. But he needed to remind himself—he had a strict no-single-mom policy in effect. And he was going to remind himself of that, every day when Grace walked through that office door.

"Here's the place," Evan said pointing to the sign that read, MY SISTER'S CLOSET. "That's the store everyone in town goes to. Well, the women anyway. It's been here since before I was born. It has everything. The only thing is." he took a deep breath and rubbed the back of his neck, "the owner is a bit crazy. So let's not dillydally in there. Because her sister is even crazier, and if she comes in—"

"Wait," Grace said, grabbing hold of his arm. He turned around, and she quickly released her hand. He was irritated that the innocuous touch sent a jolt of awareness through him. "I can't do this."

Dread gurgled in his stomach. Complicated. He knew she'd be complicated. "What do you mean?"

"I can't have you pay for a new wardrobe. It doesn't feel right, especially after you just gave me an advance. Maybe I can use that money—"

"No. This was the deal—"

"It's too much. I can't accept all of this."

He had to respect her wanting to pay. But there was no way he'd agree to that. He lowered his voice so her son couldn't hear. "What is it you object to?"

She swung her hair over her shoulder, and he knew he shouldn't notice the way the sun caught the lighter shades of brown, the way it was slightly wild. "I can't have a man just buying me clothes like I'm some charity case. I may be going through a bit of a rough time right now, but it doesn't mean I'm desperate."

Embarrassment clung to her words, and he had to respect

her pride. "Look at it as purely a business arrangement. Remember, you're the one doing *me* a favor," he said, gentling his voice. Her green eyes left his and landed on her son, who was presently leaping over sidewalk cracks. Her chin wobbled once as she stared at her kid, and his dread turned to all-out fear when he detected the possible onslaught of tears, but she pulled herself together, thankfully.

After a few moments, she nodded and then started fumbling through her giant bag. "Okay. Thank you. And let's just keep it to a minimum. I don't want anything extra. Maybe I should make a list."

He held open the door. "No time for lists. Let's go."

"Chris," she called waving her son over. "Best behavior, okay?"

His head bopped up and down.

"Come on," Evan said and took her hand. He had no idea why he did that. But he felt like she needed support. Yes, support, that must have been the reason. The feel of her soft, smaller hand in his sent a jolt straight to his gut. The bells jingled as the door closed behind them, and Grace stepped inside the colorful boutique, slowly extricating her hand from his. He didn't have time to analyze why he was disappointed that she pulled away from him, because the quiet store was suddenly bombarded by the voice that seemed to follow him wherever he went in this damn town.

"Woo-hoo! Evan Manning is that you?"

Evan swallowed his curse. Eunice Jacobs would be the death of him. He bent down to whisper in Grace's ear and was caught off guard by the scent of her shampoo or perfume or whatever it was that suddenly made him aware of her on an uncomfortable level. He forced himself to focus.

"That's the owner's crazy sister—"

"It *is* you," Mrs. Jacobs yelled in a high-pitched voice. In typical fashion, she shuffled over to them, her nutty leopard-print dress billowing out around her. Like she needed loud clothing. Evan glanced down at her foot and then looked away. He should probably ask her how she was feeling.

"And who are *you,* my dear?" The woman peered at Grace through her glasses.

Grace extended her hand and smiled as Mrs. Jacobs shook it as though it would be the last handshake of her life.

"Mrs. Jacobs, this is Grace and her son—"

Christopher poked his head out from a clothing rack. "How do you do? I'm Eunice Jacobs."

Grace gave her a warm smile. Poor, unsuspecting Grace. Someone was going to have to give her a crash course in identifying the local crazies. "Nice to meet you. This is my son, Christopher."

"We'd love to stay and chat, but we're in a hurry. We need a bunch of clothes." Evan was looking around the store, wishing for another salesperson or some act of God that might expedite what would now be a very agonizing experience. "Is there anyone else here that might be able—"

"Nope, this is your lucky day. Just me this morning filling in for Sally. You know, Christopher, I used to know Dr. Evan when he was just a baby."

Evan held his breath. Mrs. Jacobs had the capability of making grown men cry with embarrassment. He had the unsettling premonition that if he didn't stop her, he'd be one of those men in about three minutes.

"Yup, that's right," he said, flashing them a quick smile, trying to intervene before…

"And you know what else, Christopher?" Mrs. Jacobs asked, sidling up beside the boy, who seemed captivated by the woman's over-the-top screechy voice. "Once, when I was visiting Dr. Evan's mommy, Evan ran through the kitchen in just his diaper, and then tore it off—"

"Mrs. Jacobs," Evan interrupted, his throat constricting so tight he could barely speak. "We're in a big hurry. Can you please help Grace?" he asked, his teeth clenched so tight he didn't know if his words were even coherent.

"Why yes, I'll be more than glad to help out, Grace. Now, dear, the store is divided up into sections. We have everything from casual to formal and lingerie. So you just tell me what you need, and I'll advise accordingly."

"Choose the opposite of whatever she suggests," Evan whispered in her ear after Mrs. Jacobs turned. Hangers scraping against racks saved them from being heard. Mrs. Jacobs held up a neon-orange dress that looked like someone vomited ruffles and sequins all over it.

"Wow that's so cool! It's like a Halloween costume. Mommy, get that one."

Evan choked as Christopher jumped up and down.

"I'm actually looking for something a little more… subdued," Grace said, taking a small step back from the obscene gown and bumping into him. He placed his hands on her shoulders to steady her. He probably should have put distance between them, but again he was caught off guard by how good she felt. Before he could be pissed off by his growing attraction to his secretary and fake fiancée, she'd already moved away from him.

Mrs. Jacobs placed the offensive clothing back on the rack. "Well, why don't you begin by telling me what type of

events you need the clothing for?"

"A wedding, a business casual wardrobe, and a hospital gala."

"And would this wedding be *mine?*"

Grace looked over at Evan. He nodded, forcing his lips into what he thought would pass for a smile. He tuned out of the conversation, staring out the window. If either of his brothers saw him shopping for dresses with Mrs. Jacobs buzzing around, he'd never live this one down. He glanced over at Chris who was climbing through the clothing racks. Couldn't blame the kid a bit.

"…I know you're probably thinking I'm too old to get married. But I'm not. Heck, some days I still think I am young. But it's Bill that makes me feel like that. After Bill had all these health problems these last few years, we kept delaying and delaying the wedding. Finally, when we got the news that his heart just wasn't recovering as the doctors had hoped, we said, 'To hell with this! Let's just do it,'" Eunice said, the ferocity in her voice making Grace jump.

"That is one of the sweetest things I've heard. Well, congratulations, I'm so happy that I'll be a guest," she said.

"Oh, my dear we are kindred spirits, kindred! We're going to have so much fun today. I'll tell you all of Dr. Evan's little secrets while you shop."

Evan pinched the bridge of his nose. He needed some kind of divine intervention. He was even willing to ask about the foot.

His phone vibrated in his pocket. "I need to take this phone call," he said. It was Medcorp. Probably confirming their appointment for next week. He was going to be meeting with the president and VP, Bryce Lambert. Now that Grace was in the picture, it would be great to casually mention his bride-to-be and soon-to-be stepson. Since Lambert was so family-obsessed, Chalmers's practice would add to the image Evan was trying to push. He eyed the front of the store; he needed to get away from Eunice's voice and prying ears.

"I think I'll just step outside," Evan said, noting the way Grace's eyes widened. Panic. She had finally figured out Eunice was a few cards short of a full deck. He shoved his guilt aside. If she wanted to make it in Red River, she was going to have to learn how to deal with Eunice.

"Not to worry. I'll take excellent care of Grace here."

Chris attached himself to his side. "Dr. Nevan, can I go with you?" Smart kid.

"Chris, Dr. Manning has an important phone call—"

"Uh, no it's fine." He glanced down at Chris. "Just hang around where I can see you, and I'll be quick on the phone, okay?"

Christopher bopped his head up and down and obediently followed him to the front window. Evan kept an eye on the kid through his peripheral vision, while asking Bryce Lambert if he wanted to come down to Red River for their meeting. He liked this man. He shrugged off the image of Quinn and Jake's faces when he'd told them about the position. They'd never get it. Well, he didn't have to convince them. In a few weeks, he'd be back in the city and would only have to deal with their disappointment on a monthly basis.

• • •

Evan stretched out his legs on the pink armchair in the

dressing room of My Sister's Closet and tried not to fall asleep. This whole shopping thing was taking longer than he'd expected. Having a fake wife and kid was proving to be just as time-consuming as real ones. He pulled out his BlackBerry, hoping for some kind of message, voice mail, or e-mail.

"Dr. Nevan, do you have games on your phone?"

He glanced over at Chris, who was doing some coloring in a superhero notebook in the chair beside him. "No, sorry, buddy."

The little boy frowned, sort of a pensive look crossing his face. "That's okay. I begged my mom to get a phone like that, but she said it was too expensive. My friends' parents have them, and they said there are so many cool games to play."

Evan searched for something to say to him. He felt bad for them. And that was a growing sentiment, the longer he spent with Christopher and his mother. It also made him feel less guilty about pressuring Grace to go along with this farce. Because at the end of the day, she would come out ahead. She'd have a job, new clothes, expenses paid. Maybe she and her son would be able to live a better life. "Well, you know what, Chris? Maybe your mom will get a phone in the future."

"That'd be great!"

Evan shifted uncomfortably. He hoped to God he hadn't just promised this kid that Grace would buy a smart phone. He glanced over at Mrs. Jacobs, who was humming the "Wedding March" for the hundredth time in an hour as she bustled out of the room. Every five minutes or so, she would dash out to the front of the store and flash him a knowing grin. That in and of itself made him very wary. He hoped to God she wasn't trying to dress Grace up as her mini-me. That thought propelled him to stand and get a status update.

"Christopher, I'll be right back. Just stay here and color."

"No problem. I'll draw a new picture for you!"

Evan shot him a smile and walked to the dressing room. He heard the shuffling of fabric and zippers. He hesitated a moment and then knocked on the door. Surprisingly, Grace pulled the door open. And was obviously shocked that it was him standing on the other side. Probably about as shocked as he was, because frumpy Grace had just turned into the most stunning woman he'd ever seen.

He had no idea this place carried lingerie like that. If he were honest with himself, he'd acknowledge that it wasn't the lingerie; it was the woman. The black bustier she was wearing and matching, tight slip revealed curves and hollows that her baggy clothes disguised.

Grace gasped, her face turning red. "Omigod, I thought you were Mrs. Jacobs—"

"Woohoo," the woman in question trilled behind him. "Evan, where have you disappeared to?"

Shit. He glanced over his shoulder, and Grace grabbed a fistful of his shirt and yanked him into the dressing room with her. It was tiny and filled with clothes…and Grace. She was staring up at him, and her hands were splayed across his chest, and hell if all those reasons he'd just went through about why he needed to quash whatever attraction he had to her went out the window. Her breaths were coming out in rapid succession and he had the craziest urge to lean down and take her mouth under his and find out whether she tasted as sweet as she looked.

"I've rescued you," she whispered, reminding him of why he was in here. "Now I need to, um, get some clothes on."

Rescued? She'd just thrown him into a volcano of hot lava. She tried to move around him, but that movement only brought her closer, until they were plastered against each other.

Heavy footsteps only faintly registered as the feel of Grace's curvy body against his took over.

"I dropped my shirt," she hissed and then attempted to kneel down…as Mrs. Jacobs whipped open the door and screamed in their faces.

"Evan Manning, these sexy-time shenanigans may be acceptable in the city, but not in Red River. I know all about what people do in change rooms but *not* in my sister's shop. Not with an innocent little boy—"

"There are no"—he almost gagged—"*sexy-time shenanigans* going on here. It was an honest mistake," he said as he held his hand out for Grace and helped her stand.

"Mrs. Jacobs, he was just helping—"

"My dear, you are in a changing room with a man, and down on your knees. You can't be so naive in life. I know all the Manning boys, and Evan was my favorite up until this sordid escapade—"

Evan forced himself to sound calm as he stepped out of the dressing room to spare Grace more humiliation. He shut the door behind him and pointed down the hall to the waiting area where Chris was thankfully still coloring and humming loudly. "Please keep your voice down, or you'll corrupt innocent, young minds."

A few minutes later, Grace yanked open the door,

dressed and with her arms filled with clothes. She avoided looking at him as Mrs. Jacobs took the clothes from her arms. Thank God his brothers were nowhere around here. This one was going into the vault. Only problem was, he'd have to keep revisiting, because he was now aware of Grace. Every single, gorgeous curve. And the sight of her in the lace bustier and slip was carved into his head and imprinted on his body. For the first time in his life, he wished he didn't have a photographic memory.

This was exactly why he needed out of this town. Fast. He needed to land that job, get out of Red River and back to civilization. Grace needed to become just a distant memory. A sweet, hot, distant memory.

# Chapter Six

Grace took a deep breath, wrapped her hand around the cold door handle, and swung it open. The office was quiet, the fluorescent overhead lights still off. She knew Evan was inside, because the door was unlocked. She told herself that the rapid rattling in her rib cage was perfectly normal and had everything to do with the first day on a new job, and nothing to do with her employer. Especially since said employer had seen her almost naked. And she'd been pressed against all the strong lines of his body. And the look in his eyes had played over and over again in her mind the rest of the weekend.

She and Christopher had spent yesterday unpacking and doing groceries. She had made three To-Do lists and had completed two of them already. Chris could not stop speaking about Evan or the house or the yard. She felt as though she was in her dream house, it was so beautiful. Evan and everything that happened made her believe that maybe her life was finally changing. Because of him.

Grace forced what she hoped was a normal expression on her face, and not one that said, *Being smashed up against you in the dressing room was the single hottest experience of my sad little life and—*

"Oh, hey, Grace. Come on in," he said, appearing from the corridor that led to the two examination rooms. The pale blue button-down shirt and fitted navy flat-front chinos fit him to perfection. His skin was a stark contrast to the crisp white of his shirt, the khakis emphasizing his height and lean hips. He had his stethoscope looped around his neck, and his hair was slightly rumpled, giving her the impression he'd already run his hands through it a few times this morning. In a word, the man was edible. She closed her eyes briefly before she made a complete fool of herself. These were horribly inappropriate thoughts for her employer. She was fantasizing about him and he…was looking at her as though she were just another seventy-year-old receptionist. He was pure business this morning, all buttoned up and professional. The man could switch from hot casual to work casual better than anyone she'd seen.

"Thank you," she said, walking over to the brass coat rack by the receptionist's desk. She hung up her sweater and smoothed her hands over her black pencil skirt before turning to face Evan. Getting dressed this morning, she'd felt like a woman—nothing like the Ronald McDonald's sister version of herself from last week. She'd even managed to tame her crazy hair. She glanced over at Evan, but he wasn't even looking at her. He was shoving some files around on the desk, making some grumbling noises.

"Chris get off to school okay?"

Ugh. There was that other side of him. First he looked as though all he wanted was to talk about work, and then his features softened and he asked about her little boy. She was doomed. She nodded, smiling as she thought of Chris. "Like a total trooper. Honestly I don't know where he gets that confidence and outgoing personality from. If I were his age and had to switch schools and towns, I would have clung to my mother and begged her not to leave."

He was quiet for a moment, his eyes thoughtful.

"He's a pretty cool kid. He's okay with coming here after school for a couple hours every day?"

Grace placed her purse on the ground, quickly kicking it under the desk and out of sight with her fab new shoes. She hadn't wanted to add even more things to the ginormous bill Evan must have incurred on her shopping spree, so hadn't even looked in the direction of accessories that day. "Totally. And he's thrilled that he and Ella are in the same school. We ran into Holly and Ella this morning and arranged a play date this week, too. You have an incredible family; you're so lucky."

He flipped open a file. "Holly's great."

"You must be so happy to be back here, surrounded by family and old friends. I can't even imagine what it's like to have that kind of support. Well, now thanks to you, I guess I do." She tried not to get emotional, but in less than a week, these people had taken them in and shown them more kindness than anything she'd experienced before.

He gave her a terse nod, still looking in the file. It was an odd reaction. Maybe she was just babbling too long, and he wanted to get to work. Clearly, she was the only one who was having problems getting Saturday out of her mind.

"So Sheila said she left a bunch of instructions, passwords, and notes. They are in this file," he said handing it to her. She accepted it, making sure her fingers didn't touch his. "I know you have experience with this, so maybe look through all that and then ask me if you have any questions, okay? I'm not really familiar with everything around here, but I can place a call to Chalmers if needed." His eyes were intense as she sat down in the swivel chair behind the desk. "This place isn't really crazy busy this week, and the patients here are really," he paused, "easygoing, so we should be fine." Evan was all business again, a completely different man than the one a few minutes ago.

"Okay, will do," she said, anxious to have a look at everything before the first patient arrived.

"Good. I'll be in my office. Only put through work calls. My family has a habit of calling a lot just to chitchat—only put them through if it's something legit. Oh, and I am expecting an important fax from Medcorp. As soon as that comes in, please bring it to me." He left the reception room without a backward glance. She flexed her fingers and made a note of the company he'd just mentioned.

Almost an hour later, she had the computer up and running, the program the same as her old office, and was making major inroads on figuring out how everything worked.

She nearly jumped out of her seat when the phone rang, sounding shrill in the silent office. She glanced at the clock, and since it was five minutes to opening, decided she'd just pick it up.

An hour later, the doctor's office was almost filled, and she was answering calls and registering patients flawlessly. It was actually a really enjoyable morning. She basically ran the office, which she'd never been able to do in her other job, and everyone was so friendly.

# The Doctor's Fake Fiancée

When the fax finally came in just after lunch, she walked down the hall to hand it to Evan and paused, her eyes resting on the letterhead. Medcorp, private plastic-surgery clinics. And the address below was on Gerrard, downtown Toronto. It was very close to the women's shelter she and her mother had stayed at for a rough period of time. They were good people there, and when her mom had found a full-time job again and they were able to afford their own apartment, she'd made sure that the two of them volunteered as much as they could. Her mother had said it was important to be grateful, and that lesson was one Grace had never forgotten.

Her heart throbbed. She shouldn't have been reading this. But she wanted to know what it meant. She took a deep breath, eyeing the door leading to his office.

She needed this job. And she was beginning to be really hopeful for the first time in years, that she would actually be able to make it and give Christopher a good life. She wasn't about to ruin that by prying. Nope, she was going to work her butt off and impress him. In her spare time she was going to make her art a priority. She'd go back to Toronto, pull together her portfolio and all her art supplies.

Her mother would have been so proud of her. She was going to do this. She was going to make a home for herself and her son in Red River. She glanced down at the letterhead again, the logo finally triggering her memory. She frowned, looking down the hallway toward Evan's office. He couldn't possibly be leaving Red River to work *there*…

• • •

Evan was counting down the days until he could leave Red

River.

He was trying to concentrate on what Dr. Chalmers was saying during their lunch together and not on thoughts of Grace. But it'd been more than a week since she'd walked into his life, and his life had become...slightly more chaotic and complicated. He shouldn't let that bother him because, well, in a few weeks, Grace would be nothing but a distant memory. So he shouldn't be thinking about her in that lingerie. And he shouldn't be noticing her legs in the skirts she wore to work. Or the way she filled out the sweaters she wore. Or her eyes. Or her smile. Not a damn bit of it should matter because she also wasn't his type. She was too young. She was a mom. And she didn't have the career drive that he admired in all the women he'd been with—which meant she wouldn't understand his goals or the long hours he'd have to put in to achieve them. And she sure as hell wouldn't understand leaving a quaint town, a thriving family practice, to run a chain of private plastic-surgery clinics.

But then she'd do other things...like laugh with the patients. Or give her son five thousand kisses when he came back from school, even though the kid tried to wrestle free every time. And the kicker was that none of that crap should matter to Evan. But it was appealing on some level. Maybe an emotional level—the kind he'd never been aware of in himself. The kind his father had shut down from an early age. His parents had never been happy. Evan knew from a young age, marriage wasn't anything he wanted. He could control the outcome of his career—the outcome of a marriage was only 50 percent in his hands. He didn't like those odds.

"I've been thinking about retiring," Dr. Chalmers said as he took a sip from his cup of coffee.

Evan frowned, brushing aside his own inane thoughts. "Not yet. It's too soon for that, Morgan."

He chuckled, the lines in his face deepening. "I'm almost seventy-five. My wife keeps telling me I need to enjoy myself. Take some time to play with the grandchildren."

Evan looked away for a moment, out into the gardens behind his mentor. Family was the one thing they differed on. "Wouldn't you feel empty without it? You spent so much of your life building that practice."

Morgan tilted his head. "It would be an adjustment; there's no denying it. But there also comes a time when you have to realize what's more important. I've spent so long saying next year we'll do this or next year we'll do that. And you know what? We never do. None of us knows how long we're going to be here, and Pearl has put up with me for a long time. I owe her," he said with a wise smile.

Evan forced a smile in return, trying to understand. "That makes sense."

"It makes even more sense when you truly love someone. She gave up so much, being my wife. Now I think it's about time I gave something back to her. I was a workaholic, Evan. Loved my work to the point of obsession, and she tolerated it. But I'm also a smart man, and I know when it's time to throw in the towel and be the husband she deserves."

"Well, then I'm happy for you." Even if he *really* didn't get it.

Morgan chuckled. "You have no idea what the hell I'm talking about do you? Well, I hope for your sake that one day you do. This isn't everything, you know. If I had a choice between my family and practicing medicine, I'd choose my family. Remember that, and you'll be fine."

Evan nodded slowly, trying to look as though he actually thought that was good advice and would remember it—even though he'd just filed it away under useless, sentimental drivel in his mind. "So what are you going to do with the practice?"

Morgan drew a long breath and then looked him straight in the eye. "Would you be upset if I confessed and told you that I secretly hoped you'd fall in love with my patients and your hometown again, that you'd be tempted to take over?"

Evan stopped breathing for a moment. *Take over.* Be a doctor in Red River? He reached for the cup of coffee on the table in front of him and wished he could spike it with something. "I'm flattered you thought of me, but this really comes as a shock. I mean, I'd entertain the idea of family practice, maybe if I had a wife and child, if I needed to settle down. And you do have some great people." He tried to push the thoughts of all his mundane patients today out of his mind before continuing. "But I just don't know if I'm ready for that kind of commitment now. The rush of the ER would be gone. I mean the biggest rush in Red River is…" His voice trailed off, and he couldn't think of a damn thing… well he could. The biggest rush was Grace in lingerie. But he couldn't exactly say that aloud. And it was a purely normal, male reaction he surmised after thinking about her for the fiftieth time in a day. It wasn't personal.

Morgan chuckled. "True. It's a different pace. One of the biggest joys of my practice, though, is the people. You become a part of their lives. You witness the beginning of families, the birth of children, you watch them grow. I have shared in their joy and pain and I have truly helped people that I have come to care deeply for," Morgan said, his voice thick with emotion, his faded blue eyes glistening with tears.

Evan cleared his throat. The idea of what he was saying was interesting, but it also scared the hell out him. He didn't want to know people. He didn't want to get close to anyone and their families, their children. He wanted to be the best. And a small-town doctor wasn't the best.

Morgan leaned forward. "You know, rumor has it that Red River is a top contender for getting that new regional hospital."

"I didn't know that," Evan said, placing his coffee down. That interested him—mildly. But still. Red River wasn't Toronto.

"And you owe me. Didn't my secretary of thirty-five years quit after only one week with you?" Morgan asked, unruly gray eyebrows arched.

Evan shifted in his seat. "Sorry about that. I really didn't want her to leave. I think she just had some trouble keeping up."

Morgan snorted. "She came over here fit to be tied, said you were a slave driver. But I'll tell you a little something, Son, she was ready to retire, and you gave her the perfect excuse. We sort of grew old together."

"Well, I think you're going to love your new receptionist. She's extremely competent, energetic, and great with the patients. Every single person that walks into my office can't stop gushing about her." He had been shocked by that. And he didn't know how many times he'd seen Grace laughing with patients and speaking to them as though she'd known them for years.

"Good, good. I looked over the résumé you dropped off and was quite impressed. You know I trust you. I also think how nice — a new secretary and a new doctor... I'm sure those brothers of yours would love to have you back in town with them. And what about your adorable nephew and niece?"

Evan ducked his head. Of course he missed Jake and Quinn. And his sisters-in-law. And the kids. But he saw them fairly often anyway, even when he'd worked in the city. He didn't need to seem them *every single day.* "You know how to hit hard, don't you, Morgan?"

"And your parents, they would have loved to see you as a family doctor in their beloved town," Morgan pushed.

Evan grit his teeth. No, his father would have said that practicing medicine in a tiny town like Red River wasn't good enough. The only thing that would be good enough was being the best. The top.

Morgan smiled, taking another sip of his coffee. "I'm sensing it's now or never for you. I made a promise to myself — I wouldn't retire if I didn't have complete confidence in the new doctor. I owe these people, and I love them, and I can't leave them under the care of just anyone. I need a doctor with heart," he said.

Evan didn't know how to tell his friend the person he was describing was not him. He had no idea how Morgan would have ever thought Evan would be the right replacement. He stared out the window, trying to feel the impact of what Morgan had told him. And he couldn't.

"As much as I'd like to be, I'm not your man. I'm pretty much a shoo-in for heading up the new Medcorp clinics."

Morgan's white brows snapped together violently. "What?"

Evan nodded. He knew this wouldn't go over well.

"I'd worked with Lambert in the past, and the opportunity practically fell into my lap—"

"But plastic surgery in a private clinic? Evan?"

Evan leaned forward in his chair. There was nothing anyone could say to sway him from his goal. He wanted this position at Medcorp. The meeting with Lambert needed to go flawlessly. By the time he walked into the gala, his position as CEO would be secure. "I've wanted this for a long time. I know you may not agree—"

"Of course I don't agree. How satisfying will your career be? You still wouldn't be a surgeon. Is that really what you want? Is that what you dreamed of doing?"

Evan ripped his gaze from Chalmers and looked out the window. "Morgan, with all due respect, this is a career move that will give me back some of what I lost—"

"Ah, so this is about ego. The brilliant surgeon at the top of his game is desperately trying to be at the top again. Well, speaking from the mouth of an old man who's made many mistakes, I'll tell you this—smoke and mirrors. That job will bring you no fulfillment. It'll line your pockets, but you will never be emptier. You will be nothing like the young boy that came into my office every day. Nothing like the young boy who tried to rescue all sorts of insects and animals. You wanted to heal. That job will take you away from your roots, from the beliefs that I know you still have somewhere deep inside, Evan Manning."

# Chapter Seven

Grace crossed "buy new purse and portfolio for gallery interview" off her To-Do list. She'd managed that purchase on her lunch break today. Now all she needed was to get through the actual interview. And if that interview went as well as Evan's was no doubt going right now, she would have fulfilled one of her biggest goals.

She almost fell off her chair as a pounding on the front door shattered the silence in the quiet office. She looked over at Christopher who was seated in one of the waiting-room chairs playing a game Evan had downloaded for him on his phone. Grace had been shocked when he'd handed Chris his phone and told him he could use it for the duration of his meeting with the man from Medcorp. And then of course she'd added "smart phone" to the growing list of things she was going to soon be able to afford, thanks to this job. When she'd tried hinting at more information about Evan's involvement with Medcorp, he'd just evaded the question. He just said he was entertaining a new career option. It hadn't been her place to ask. And it reminded her of her role here—fake fiancée and receptionist. Nothing more.

She frowned and glanced at the clock on the wall, when the knocking grew louder and even Chris was drawn from his intense concentration.

She glanced down the hallway—Evan's office door was still closed. His important meeting was in full swing, and so far, Chris had behaved wonderfully. She'd been nervous about having the meeting run so late and overlapping with Christopher's time at the office. But Evan had reassured her that Mr. Lambert was a family man, so her son would be welcome. Still, it was imperative nothing went wrong and that she made a good impression. She needed to act like she thought Evan's fiancée would act: sophisticated, intelligent, and slightly anal.

"Who's that, Mom?"

Grace groaned. "I have no idea." She jogged over to the front door when the pounding continued. A young man in jeans and a checked shirt was standing there. His face was red, and beads of sweat dripped down his acne-marred face. His thin arms were weighted down by large cages in each hand. Grace's eyes widened as she recognized chickens inside the cages.

"Chickens!" Christopher whispered loudly…and with reverence.

Oh, this was going to be bad. Her Spidey-senses were tingling. She squeezed her eyes shut praying for a second that he'd just go away. She jumped when he banged on the door again. Nope. He definitely didn't go away.

She unlocked the door, and the man began frantically

speaking in a rather high-pitched voice, "You gotta help me. My truck died right outside, and it's a freaking heat wave today. I called the mechanic, and it'll take him at least half an hour to get out here. I can't leave the chickens back there for that long. They'll die." He held up the cages and thrust one in her direction.

She took a step back and shoved Chris behind her as he made an attempt to grab a cage. "I'm sorry, but—"

"Please just help me get the cages into your place. I'm filling in for my brother, and he'll get fired if I screw this up—"

"I can't," she said, looking over her shoulder, grateful that Evan hadn't heard any of the commotion.

Chris wrapped himself around her calf. "Mom, you have to—"

"This is a doctor's office. What about trying one of the other—"

"I have. Everything is closed already, except the restaurants, and they won't take in animals!" The young man's voice was climbing higher and higher. He was right. Weekdays in downtown Red River meant everything closed early. She squeezed the door handle. She couldn't allow this man to bring in chickens to the office. Especially today of all days.

He dangled a cage in her face, and the poor chicken made a panicked *cluuuuuuuck*. Grace squeezed her eyes shut. She couldn't do this. What would Evan's fiancée do? She racked her brain frantically… Evan's fiancée would politely shut the door and lock it. Then she would tell Evan over some candlelight dinner about her brilliant disaster aversion skills, and he'd thank her profusely for not caving like an idiot and letting chickens into Chalmers's practice during the most important meeting of his career.

# The Doctor's Fake Fiancée

Grace hung her head as the clucking increased in volume. She was caving like said idiot. She couldn't very well just allow innocent animals to scorch in the heat while she sat in the nicely cooled doctor's office.

"Please, lady, I just need you to help me out until the mechanic gets here and can get the AC working in my truck. It's been out for over two hours. I need to get them cooled down. It won't be long. I'll get out of your way real fast."

Maybe it was the panic in his eyes. This man was all alone, and he needed help. How many times had she been alone and in need? Surely Evan would understand. He had, after all, saved her and her son from a burning car. He couldn't just stand by and let the chickens die. Grace took a deep breath and opened the door wider. "Okay listen, you get the chickens from the truck, and I'll give you twenty minutes. That's it, or I'll be the one who's fired," she hissed.

"Deal. Thanks, lady!"

The young man ran to his truck, and Grace glanced down at her son. He was grinning at her with a mix of adoration and anticipation.

Ten minutes later, she drummed her fingers on her desk. She picked her pen up, waiting to cross off "Get chickens out of office before your ass is toast" from her list. Her gaze darted in regular intervals between the chickens, the clock, her list, and her son. Chris was pacing the cages and then peeking down the hallway for her. Every so often, he'd give her the thumbs-up, indicating Evan's office door hadn't opened.

She reached for her third tissue in minutes, anticipating a sneeze. She had a sneaking suspicion she was allergic to chickens. After sneeze number five, Evan's office door creaked open, and Christopher whispered a frantic, "*Mom.*"

Crap. She was toast. She bolted around the corner of her desk, not really knowing what the hell she was going to do. Evan was going to kill her. Or fire her. Or both. She yanked Christopher over to her, and they stood in front of the dozen chicken cages, stoically, as though there was a chance in holy hell that Evan or Mr. Lambert weren't going to notice that the pristine office had now been turned into some sort of farm-animal rescue center.

"Don't worry, Mom. Dr. Evan is really cool and — "

Even Christopher knew he should stop talking when Evan and Lambert appeared in the doorway. Evan's victorious smile melted faster than soft-serve ice cream in a heat wave. He closed his eyes for a second, and Grace presumed he was hoping that when he opened them again, this would all be some sort of nightmare. She smiled feebly when his eyes opened, and he looked at the cages that were still there and then at her.

It was not the same look he'd given her when they'd been locked in the changing room.

The dense, frantic flapping of wings reverberated through the empty office. Grace tried to open her mouth, but her voice failed her. Instead frantic clucking began. Christopher slapped his hands over his face and shook his head. She heard him mumble "*Doomed.*"

Grace cleared her throat. "I…um, there was a bit of an emergency situation — "

Her son stepped forward heroically. "Mom's a chicken-rescuer. They were all going to explode from a fiery truck — "

Grace knew the only one who was going up in flames was her at this moment. She wrapped her arm around Chris, her hand patting his overly chatty mouth until he stopped talking. Dr. Lambert frowned, his gaze following something above her. Grace looked up and swallowed her scream. She jetted her arm out to capture the feather floating in the air. She didn't dare look over at Evan.

"Where is this burning truck?" Evan asked, his voice sounding thick and strained. And so *very, very*, pissed.

Grace cleared her throat. "It's not *exactly* on fire—"

"The chicken man is back!" Christopher yelled as the young man whipped open the door. She breathed a sigh of relief.

She took a step forward. "Dr. Manning, Dr. Lambert, I'm so sorry for the mess... I just couldn't stand by and let these...innocent chickens die."

"Thanks, lady," the man said, quickly grabbing a few cages. Christopher ran over to hold open the door for him. Evan hadn't moved. Not a square inch of that hard body had so much as twitched. But Lambert was grinning and watching her.

"Well, we all have to do our part in this world, don't we?" he said with a hearty chuckle.

Grace breathed a sigh of relief as the older man winked at her. "Grace it has been a pleasure meeting with you and your son. Evan," he said, extending his hand, "this visit has been an enlightening one for me. Thank you. I'll be in touch."

Grace gave him her most professional smile and tried not to gasp in horror as the young man almost crashed into Mr. Lambert with one of the cages. Once Mr. Lambert left the building Grace walked over to Evan who still hadn't moved. "Evan, I'm so sorry—"

"Lady, thanks again for helping me out. You saved my

butt and my brother's. I knew it was going to be a bad day when I pressed snooze on my alarm."

Evan looked over her shoulder to address the young man. "If you value employment, I suggest you don't press snooze."

The young man's face grew a deep red. He backed up a step and nodded quickly, scrambling to retrieve the last cage. Evan stared the man down, and Grace took a step back from Evan's scary-controlled-but-enraged body. The second the door shut behind him, Grace told Christopher to sit down and play a game quietly. Chris glanced at Evan then at Grace and quickly nodded.

"Evan," she whispered as he began walked down the hallway, away from the waiting room. He slowed and she caught up with him, her hand on his arm. "I'm sorry."

He looked down at her, and she swallowed hard. He was gorgeous up close. The blue in his eyes became more intense... Then again, that could have been because they were filled with carefully controlled anger. The lines of his perfectly chiseled face, the premium bone structure was even more enticing with the five-o'clock shadow he was sporting. Or it could just be the fact that the premium bone structure was being highlighted by the rhythmic clenching and unclenching of his jaw.

"You do realize those chickens were in that truck most likely on their way to the slaughterhouse—"

She shook her head vehemently. "No—"

Evan rubbed the back of his neck and stared at the ceiling for a minute. "Yes. Why else was this guy driving a bunch of chickens around? You didn't save their feathered asses; you just prolonged their agony."

She sputtered out a huff and then lifted her chin. "I did what I felt I needed to."

"Fine, Grace, fine. You did what you needed to, and so did I. I've got at least an hour's worth of test results to look through. Good night." He turned around in the direction of his office. She squeezed her eyes tightly shut. She had royally screwed up. She had been hired to help him out, not add to his problems. And whether or not the man lacked compassion for chickens, he was her employer. There was nothing stopping him from canning her. And then where would she and Christopher be?

"Evan?"

He stopped, but didn't turn around.

She cleared her throat. "You're, um, not going to fire me are you?"

There was a brief pause, during which she didn't dare breathe.

"I can't very well fire my fiancée, can I?"

And then he walked away, leaving her in the midst of the feather-filled waiting room.

• • •

He was being an ass. But the second he'd seen those chickens squawking around the waiting room, all he could think was how he'd just blown this opportunity with Medcorp. And after his meeting with Lambert, he'd thought it was practically a done deal. They got along well, saw eye to eye on how the clinics should be run, and Evan knew in his gut he was the top contender. Lambert loved family through and through, and he wanted a man who had the same beliefs.

Evan fit the bill—personally and professionally.

And then when they'd walked out...to see how unprofessionally the office was being run, Evan had been pissed. But now he was more pissed at himself. Or Red River. Yes. He'd blame it on being back here and all these people screwing with his plans. A couple weeks ago, there had been no complications. He knew he wanted to be the CEO of Medcorp. He wanted out of Red River. He'd achieve his new career goals, and he'd be happy. Done. Now...now lines were being crossed and blurred. Now, he wondered if his career goals were merely prompted by some subconscious need to be the best for his father. But he loathed his father now that he knew the truth, so following his words...didn't make sense.

He swore, stood up and shoved the swivel chair hard across the room, watching numbly as it crashed into the examination table. He contemplated kicking it, but he was wearing the wrong shoes for that. He needed to go for a run and then find his brothers and have a few beers on one of their back porches. He swung around as a knock sounded. He frowned. It couldn't still be Grace. He assumed she'd left after his asshole behavior.

Grace pried opened the always-sticky door a second later, poking her head in first. Probably trying to make sure he wasn't in some sort of crazy-person rage.

"I didn't know you were still here," he said.

Her lips pursed, and she raised her eyebrows. "I was just cleaning up a few stray feathers."

He ducked his head as the urge to laugh threatened. He'd almost thought Grace would have been crying over how he'd acted. Instead she kinda looked pissed off at him...

and he was relieved by that.

"And for the record, I really am sorry that the whole chicken debacle happened during your appointment with Lambert, but I still stand by my decision to save the chickens." She folded her arms primly in front of her and took a deep breath. He took in the sudden appearance of cleavage with her movement. It was the nicest damn sight all day. *Grace* was becoming the nicest sight at the end of every day.

He raised his gaze to her eyes, only to find them narrowed into little slits. Right. She was in the process of justifying letting dozens of chickens in. "It was what any decent human being would have done."

Which implied she doubted his decency. For some reason, the need to change her opinion of him suddenly mattered. "Well...we all have to stand by our principles. And for the record, you don't have to be worried about your job. You're essential here. I wouldn't be able to keep up if it weren't for you."

Her expression softened, and judging by the way her shoulders relaxed, he'd just alleviated her fears. He really had been an ass. "Okay, I guess I'll just finish tidying up the kitchen and be out of here."

He started gathering his papers from his desk and stuffing them into his bag. "Why do you need to tidy up the kitchen? Cleaners come in every night."

He glanced over at her when she didn't answer.

"Haven't you been in there lately?"

He shook his head. Usually coffee magically appeared on his desk throughout the day. And he never bothered bringing a lunch to work, just skipped out for a sandwich at Nat's bakery and café. Sometimes if he was behind schedule—usually due to someone insisting on asking him questions about his personal life—the bakery would send someone over with takeout. And in typical Red River fashion, there was always something slightly wonky about his order—like someone had helped themselves to the chips on the side of the sandwich. "No, why?"

Her long-winded sigh had him distracted by her cleavage again. She walked forward and grabbed him by the wrist, yanking him down the hall. And as usual, the feel of Grace's soft skin sent an electrical jolt through his system. And, as usual, he pushed it aside because it was an irrelevant reaction because he and Grace could never be anything more than their fake relationship.

They stood in the doorway of the small kitchenette. She raised her brows and tilted her head in the direction of the room. He was obviously supposed to be noticing something. When he didn't answer, she nudged him in the ribs and then pointed to the counter. It was filled with plates of desserts covered in plastic wrap.

He frowned. "What's with the buffet?"

She rolled her eyes. "Are you serious? Your patients have been bringing all this in for weeks."

He searched for the right words. "My patients clearly have issues with sugar."

"It's a way for them to let you know how happy they are to have you back in town. They adore you, Evan."

Evan leaned against the doorjamb and crossed his arms. He scanned the food, kind of incredulous. Maybe even touched, not that he wanted to be. He hadn't planned on being affected by anyone in Red River. He narrowed his eyes on a familiar plate with cellophane and a big bow. He

clenched his teeth. He was an ass. He'd never even bothered looking at one of those muffins she'd brought.

"Well, I'd better get going. I was going to mention… before the whole chicken debacle, that I have been taking notes since I started here about how we can improve things. I think I have some pretty good ideas—"

"Sure. I'd love to hear them."

She gave him a bright smile. "Okay, maybe tomorrow morning?"

His gaze fell to her lips. "How about dinner tonight?"

She tucked a few strands of hair behind her ear, but the curls fell back out. Without thinking twice, he reached out and tucked them behind her ear. Her breath caught, and a flicker of recognition passed through her eyes. And he realized he wanted more than a flicker, more than recognition. He wanted to see desire. Dammit if that wasn't the worst thought right now.

She stepped back, bumping into the wall. He put his hands in his pockets to keep himself from tugging her over to him. "Um, actually I'm busy tonight. Chris and I are going to Holly and Quinn's for dinner."

He blinked. His family hadn't invited him. He tossed that thought aside. He shouldn't care. Really. "I'm glad you and Holly get along so well." He was. Inexplicably pleased that she seemed to be fitting in so well to this town…and his family.

She smiled up at him earnestly. "Me, too. Maybe we can try that new vegan restaurant at lunch? I think they have big tables, so we can spread out our files."

He opened his mouth, fully intending on saying yes, but then snapped it shut. Jake's idiotic face popped into his mind, along with his advice not to order salad on dates with women. But this wasn't a date. This was Grace, his receptionist. *His hot-in-lingerie receptionist. His single-mom receptionist. His bleeding-heart, chicken-rescuing fiancée...* He tried his hardest to internally recite his anti-single-mom policy, but when Grace looked up at him, large green eyes filled with... the emotion that he had managed to run from his entire life, he couldn't think of one damn reason to not want Grace. "So tomorrow night?"

She winced. "Tomorrow night we're going to Jake and Claire's."

Well, hell. She patted him on the arm and gave him the same sympathetic smile she gave to Christopher when he fell down riding his bicycle last week. "Maybe Friday?"

# Chapter Eight

"Thanks for squeezing me in at the last minute on a Friday, sweetheart," Mr. McCann called out in his gravelly voice, limping and managing to wink as he emerged from the hallway.

Evan had almost forgotten they weren't alone in the building. His eyes widened as the elderly man attempted to lean against the desk as though he were forty years younger and had a chance in hell at picking up a woman like Grace. Evan bit down on his tongue and resisted the urge to tell the man that pose wasn't the best considering his approaching hip-replacement surgery. No, instead Evan stood there watching as Grace laughed and joked as she wrote down the time of his next appointment.

But when Mr. McCann got a nice eyeful as Grace leaned over to help him with his cane and her shirt gaped, revealing some pale pink lace he knew he hadn't purchased at My Sister's Closet, Evan decided that was enough. He slapped the man on the back, a little too hard it seemed, as Grace gasped. "We'll see you next week, Mr. McCann. Try and give that hip some rest."

The man turned to scowl at him, bushy gray brows snapping down like one of those Muppet characters in the critique balcony.

"You bet, Grace," he said as though Evan hadn't spoken at all. Evan didn't bother mentioning that he was the one who actually conducted the examination, not Grace. But, whatever. This behavior was something he was seeing more and more of. Every time he came out of his office during the day, Grace was laughing and joking with everyone. He wouldn't be surprised if she already knew their entire patient list by first name.

He followed Mr. McCann to the front door and locked it behind him. He turned to Grace who was standing by the fax. He wasn't going to check her out from behind like he was some creepy-ass boss. So he refused to process how good she looked in the narrow black pencil skirt and high heels.

He cleared his throat. "So, why don't I pick you up around seven?"

She spun around to look at him. "Oh, I assumed we were just going to go there now."

Right. Because it wasn't a date. It was an after-work meeting that she had suggested.

But he wanted to take her out to a nice place. Sit across the table from her and listen. He wanted to find a reason to not like Grace so much. Yes, that was it. Maybe by the end of the night he'd be so bored out of his mind that all these inconvenient feelings he was having would finally be quashed. "Well, I thought you deserved a nice dinner out. You've been doing an amazing job around here, and it's the least I could do."

A gorgeous shade of pink swept over her face, and her full lips pulled into a smile. "Thank you. Well," she began tucking and sorting some papers until they were neat on the desk, "I think that will work because Ella asked if Chris could go over and watch some new movie at their house tonight. I was just planning on making some To-Do lists and doing laun"—she coughed turned a few shades pinker— "relaxing for the evening."

He stifled his grin. He'd seen her with that Spider-Man notepad around the office and everywhere she went. He held open the door for her once she'd gathered her things. "So I'll pick you up at your house at seven."

"Right. Great."

He turned to lock the door and she was still there, awkwardly in the crook of his arm. And the second their proximity registered, she backed up a step.

"See ya."

• • •

Grace gripped the open doors of her closet, trying desperately to choose something appropriate for her date— *no, meeting*—with Evan.

"Mom! Our friends are here!" Christopher yelled from his room. They weren't expecting anyone.

By the time she made it downstairs, Chris had already opened the door and Holly, Claire, Ella, and Michael were standing in the entryway.

"Sorry I didn't call first. I know you were going to drop Christopher off, but I just got some awesome news and couldn't wait. Since we were all out, we thought we'd drop by, and then I can take Christopher home," Holly said placing her bag on the front table.

Grace moved aside, ushering them all in. She tried not to jump to conclusions about the news. "Thanks, Holly! Good news?"

"Can we go play?"

Grace nodded as Ella and Christopher bounded up the stairs. Grace's heart was pounding as she waited for Holly to spill it.

"The gallery called. You've got an appointment set up— two weeks from now!" She handed Grace a slip of paper with the exact time and date. Grace stared at the paper and then back up at Holly.

"Thank you," she said, choked up. She couldn't believe this. Everything that had happened to her since meeting Evan was…like a miracle. She had a job that was actually pleasant, well-paying, a beautiful home, her son loved his new school and had tons of friends, and now…a chance at making her dream come true with her artwork. If she could hold onto the job at the family practice and then still have time to paint and sell some pieces of art, her finances would finally start to improve. This break she was getting on rent would allow her to bank some money for the first time in her life. She'd be able to set aside money for Christopher; they could have security. She reached out and flung her arms around Holly. "Thank you," she whispered again.

Holly pulled back after a few moments, smile still in place. "You're so welcome, I'm so happy I could do this for

you."

"Congratulations," Claire said. "I can't wait to see your work."

"So, um, what are your plans for tonight?" Claire shifted Michael to her other hip, her eyes locked on Grace even though the eighteen month old was squirming.

She totally adored Evan's sisters-in-law, and she'd never had friends like them. Ever. But she was reluctant to mention her...attraction to Evan. Something was telling her not to spill it. "You know, I was just trying to pick out something to wear because Evan will be here in like an hour. Do you want to come upstairs? Claire, you can bring Michael up and he can play in my room. It's all carpeted."

"Perfect," Holly said as they made their way up the stairs. "So is this a *date*?"

Grace tried to walk and talk and not fall flat on her butt as she thought of going on a date with Evan. "No, no. Just a work thing—"

"But you're stressing about what to wear?" Claire asked, as they walked into Grace's room. She had her there.

Claire settled on the plush carpeting as Michael attempted walking, and Holly sat on the edge of the four-poster bed.

"Where are you going for dinner?" Claire asked, catching Michael before he slammed his head against the dresser.

Grace walked over to her closet. "I'm not sure exactly. He said something about a place in Port Ryan?" Grace turned around when she heard a squeal from Holly. She pointed to both of them. "It's not what you think, trust me—"

"Oh sweetie, we know Ev. Better than Evan knows himself, because we're married to his brothers. And even though he thinks he's so different from them, there are certain similarities that just can't be ignored. Trust us when we say that Evan is very interested in you."

Grace's jaw was hanging open at Holly's declaration. She was about to argue when Claire cut her off, Michael dangling off the side of her shoulder. "Their father did a number on them, not that Evan will admit it, but trust me when I say he's a good man who is really, really smart in his professional life, but really dumb when it comes to his personal. He actually thinks he's perfectly happy in Toronto. And he thinks he's not a family man—which is a total lie because even when he was living in Toronto, our doorbell would ring at like ten o'clock at night and it would be him with a six-pack, still in his hospital scrubs, and ready to watch the rest of the hockey game with Quinn and Jake. He's always picking up little gifts for the kids, and he even plays dolls with Ella. He just needs the right woman to make him realize that. That Alexandra witch he was with—"

"—did him the biggest favor by ditching him. You are *exactly* what Evan needs—"

Grace looked back and forth between them. They were wrong. Even though she thought it was adorable that Evan was so sweet to his niece and nephew—which she could totally see because he'd been great with Christopher—it didn't make him boyfriend or father material. She was curious about the father and Alexandra mention, though. Finally she held up her hands. "We're not like that. I just work for him. I'm helping him out, but that's it. I mean, I owe the man. I wouldn't be alive if it weren't for him. But I know for a fact, I'm not his type…but, um," she walked over to sit beside Holly on the bed. She thought of the entire chicken debacle and how it all went down. So not Evan's type. She

cleared her throat. "What's with this Alexandra woman?"

Claire narrowed her eyes. "Let's just say this woman—who was a surgeon, too—dumped his cute behind after the accident."

"He totally pretended like it was no big deal. But it was. Evan was one of those kid geniuses who skipped a bunch of grades and was obsessed with getting ahead, working constantly."

"And she dumped him? Why?"

"Because he wasn't *good* enough for her anymore."

Grace flung herself back on the bed. "Seriously? Evan should hate me. Pulling us out of the car cost him his career as a surgeon and his girlfriend."

"No you didn't, sweetie. You're just what Evan needs. I've always believed that everything happens for a reason. Sometimes we can't see what the reason is, but there is good in anything if you look hard enough."

Grace ran her hands down her face. "Holly, that's a really nice theory—"

"Don't even bother arguing with her, Grace. Holly gives everyone that piece of advice."

"It's solid advice. Besides, you can't argue with a hormonal pregnant lady."

She had her there. Grace slowly sat up, Holly and Claire smiling at her. "Okay. No arguing but I just want to be clear that there's nothing going on between Evan and I. He asked me to do him this favor and pretend to be his fiancée for this gala—"

"Ugh. Medcorp," Claire said. She gave Michael a kiss on his head as the toddler finally settled in her lap, resting his head on her shoulder. Grace wanted to ask them what made them so sure Evan was wrong. The man was extremely confident and intelligent. He obviously knew what he wanted. She didn't understand what was so horrible about the position at Medcorp. The more she thought about it after Mr. Lambert's visit, the more she came up with plausible reasons a man like Evan would have for working at Medcorp. Why were they so against his new career aspirations?

She was about to ask when Holly gasped. "We've blabbed way too long. Evan is going to be here in thirty minutes. What are you wearing?"

Grace bolted from the bed, and the three of them examined the contents of her closet.

Half an hour later, they all agreed that an aqua, knee-length sundress with spaghetti straps would be ideal for wherever Evan was taking her. Strappy white three-inch wedges and a short white, short-sleeved cardigan tied the look together.

"Hair up or down?" Grace asked, half an hour later, standing in front of the floor-length mirror at the front door. Her makeup was applied, she was dressed, and she had just engaged in the most hilarious sixty minutes of female conversation she'd ever had in her adult life. She had just found out more insider info on Evan than she had working with him the last few weeks. She'd almost forgotten about Evan's ex and everything he'd faced after the accident.

"Down," Claire said with authority.

Grace smiled at her through the reflection in the mirror. "Are you sure it's not a little too crazy-looking?"

"Are you kidding? I'd love to have curly hair. It's gorgeous."

"You're beautiful. Absolutely perfect. Ugh, I can't wait

until I can wear normal clothes again," Holly groaned, rubbing her stomach.

Grace smiled. "Well, for what it's worth, you do look great. Especially since you're so close."

"Thanks. Now it's all nerves setting in. I'm kind of freaking out that I won't be able to do this."

"You'll be fine," Claire said, giving her a little hug. "If I can have a baby, so can you, Holly."

Grace tried not to look nosy, but she thought it was an odd comment for Holly to make, considering this baby would be her second child. But she wasn't about to ask, so she just stood there awkwardly.

"Oh I'm sorry, Grace," Holly said.

"For what?"

"I guess I assumed Evan had said something. But then again, he's not really the type to bring up personal things."

"That's okay. I don't want to pry—"

"Ella isn't my biological daughter. She was my sister Jennifer's daughter. When Ella was a few months old, Jennifer and her husband were in a fatal car accident."

Grace couldn't help the gasp that escaped her lips, and she covered her mouth with her hand, tears filling her eyes. "I'm so sorry."

Holly smiled softly, tears making her own eyes shimmer. "Thank you. I came back to Red River, planning on cutting ties with everything here, including Quinn. But instead, I learned a lot about myself. And Quinn, and the fact that those Mannings won't give up on the women they love. I fell in love with him and Ella. And we adopted her. It was a horrible tragedy what happened to Jen and her husband, but I thank God every day that Ella was spared and is with us."

Grace gave Holly a hug and the three of them stood there crying and smiling.

"Maybe I should come back later," Evan said, startling all of them. Despite the expression of horror at seeing them crying, he looked like every single fantasy she'd ever had about the perfect man. His hair was still slightly damp, dark and delicious. In some other world, she would have loved to walk over to him and greet him with a kiss. And he'd kiss her back until her knees went weak…

Claire yanked him in. "Get back here, Evan. Tears are gone, no need to run."

They all burst out laughing.

•  •  •

"This is so pretty," Grace said, trying not to gasp and look like a woman who'd never been to a nice restaurant. The drive over had been slightly awkward, as she processed everything Claire and Holly had said to her about him. But then she'd glance down at the files poking out of her bag; this was a business meeting. And she would not think of him in any other way than her employer. But that had been difficult as almost everything he did had her stomach flip-flopping. The way he shifted gears, the way his profile looked so stoic, the ways his eyes crinkled at the corners, the deep voice that was filled with confidence.

Oh she was toast, she realized as he'd opened her door and led her to the historic restaurant inside an old mill. The light touch of his fingers at the small of her back as they walked to their table was enough to send goose bumps filling every square inch of skin.

They were seated at a little table by the window. The view of the rushing water from the mill set off the pristine white tablecloth and china and silverware. It almost made her feel like she and Evan were on a date. She studied his face as he settled into his seat; the perfectly chiseled features, the way his shirt clung to his broad shoulders. And then she remembered: he would never be on a date with her. Grace glanced down at the file beside her. This was why they were out tonight: work. She needed to remember that before she made a fool of herself and started drooling like a woman who hadn't been out with a man in five years. Which was all true of course, but she didn't need to look it. She should look like a woman who went out with a man like Evan every week — or at least once a year. She straightened her back; she should also look as though she went out to restaurants like this. She glanced down at her unmanicured nails and curled her fingers into a fist on her lap. Who was she kidding? Her tell-all kid had basically revealed that for at least one night in their lives, they'd been homeless.

Grace reached for the file, but Evan stopped her. He raised his hand, slowly taking the file from her hand and set it down on the window ledge beside him.

"Why don't we order some wine, look at the menu, and forget about the office for a while?"

Charming. Handsome. Courteous. *Don't go reading more into that gleam in those gorgeous blue eyes.* "Sure," she said, opening the leather bound menu. She was going to have to let him choose the wine, because the last bottle she'd ever bought was called Fat Bastard, and it had been in the clearance section.

Grace glanced at the fine black print, almost every

single dish appealing to her. "According to Quinn, this place has the best beef tenderloin in the region. Considering my brothers only eat food that's been slaughtered, I trust their opinion."

Grace smiled as she closed her menu. "I think I'll have the same. I definitely won't be having the chicken," she said under her breath. Evan's deep chuckle had her curling her toes and smiling along with him.

Once they'd placed their orders Grace took a sip of her wine as Evan sat back in his chair, calm, confident. The exact opposite of herself at the moment.

"You must be so happy to be around your brothers every day. Your entire family is so sweet. This must be like a dream come true. I'm sure when you're in Toronto you'll be wishing you were back in Red River."

Evan coughed—or choked—on his wine before he answered. "It's…a change of pace, definitely. But I don't see Red River as my home anymore."

A vague uneasiness swept through her. Maybe it was intuition, reminding her of the mistakes she'd made before, trusting Brian. She had stayed away from men for years, so why was she starting to fall for the one man who was clearly focused on career only? She needed to remember what all the men in her life reiterated before they walked out the door: *I'm sorry, this just wasn't what I signed up for.* How could that have happened to her twice? The only answer she had was that the problem was her. Her father had walked out, and Brian had walked out. Love should have been enough to make anything work. And obviously, neither of them had loved her enough. She wasn't strong enough to go through that again. *Remember that, Grace.*

She toyed with the napkin in her lap and focused on answering the question as nonchalantly as she could. "Oh. Well, I guess I'm not surprised, I mean I know you told me about going back to the city when Dr. Chalmers was better. I must have assumed…I don't know what I thought really. You just seem so close to your family." She felt like an idiot. Here she was assuming what the man loved and didn't love. She didn't know anything about his likes and dislikes. "I'd love to have a family like them. Your niece and nephew. And Holly and Claire…" Her voice trailed off as Evan just shifted in his seat and drank more wine.

"They are great. All of them. Staying in Red River wasn't part of my plan."

She tried to shrug off the disappointment she had no business feeling. It shouldn't matter to her what Evan was planning on doing. Even if Holly and Claire thought there might be something between them.

She needed to focus on her art—especially considering the break Holly had just given her—and reestablishing a life for herself in this small town. And after just a short amount of time, she felt more at home here than she ever had since her mother had died.

Evan's eyes narrowed on something behind her, and he muttered a few words under his breath. Grace frowned, turning in the direction of his stare. She smiled as she spotted Mr. and Mrs. Puccini and waved at them.

He leaned forward. "Why are you waving?"

"What do you mean?"

"I try not to encourage too many conversations outside the practice—"

Grace started to laugh, thinking he was joking. She'd

gotten used to his dry humor these last few weeks. But he didn't laugh at all. The man was serious. "They are so sweet—"

"Sweet is the problem. Did you see what that waitress just brought them? Some thousand-layer concoction of chocolate and icing. Mr. Puccini is on the verge of having to go on insulin for Type II diabetes. I just spent twenty minutes—which is ten minutes longer than I should have spent—lecturing him on how a few diet changes would make a big difference in staving off the progression of his condition." He looked over his shoulder. "I should really go over there and yank that plate—"

"You will do no such thing."

"Excuse me?"

"It's their fiftieth wedding anniversary tonight. Yesterday, after their appointment they stayed and chatted with me. They also brought in some cannoli; I guess you didn't see." She quickly moved on from the cannoli when Evan's brows snapped together at the mention of more dessert. "Seriously, Evan. This is a huge milestone—"

"If they want to celebrate any more milestones together, they should lay off the dessert. I should talk to Natalia about making them stay away from the bakery."

"She's their daughter. She can't ban them." She leaned down, reaching for her file with notes. This time, Evan didn't stop her. Obviously, Holly and Claire were wrong. Evan had no interest in her other than as his secretary.

• • •

*You're toast, Evan.* His attraction to Grace hadn't waned. It had increased exponentially as she sat across the table from him. He had sat and behaved like a blubbering fool, watching the way the candlelight picked up the different shades of brown and gold in her hair. The way she laughed, throwing back her head every now and then. And then he'd noticed the expanse of perfect, creamy skin and wondered if it was as soft as it looked. He even liked the way she frowned at him, eyes flashing as he reprimanded his dessert-obsessed patients. But he'd made a promise to Grace that first day at the clinic—he wouldn't let Chris get attached. He needed to remember that. He didn't want to hurt either of them. Grace needed someone good in her life. A guy that would make her and Christopher first. And he knew that sleeping with her wasn't an option. For her anyway. She was a woman who wanted commitment. Commitment to anything other than his career wasn't an option for him.

They were walking down Main Street, Port Ryan. It was still early in the season, and the tourist attractions hadn't opened yet. It occurred to him that in all the time they'd spent together, he'd learned very little about her. He didn't know anything about her as a person. This bond she'd suddenly formed with his sisters-in-law was slightly disconcerting because those two knew everything about him. And he knew they both loved Grace, which could only mean they were encouraging something that could never happen between him and Grace. He'd never told them anything about his phobia of single mothers. Or Red River. Or anything that involved the institution of marriage.

He knew Holly was helping Grace with her art. What kind of art, he had no idea. Hell, he'd never been into that scene, and he wouldn't know where to even begin. He had no idea if Grace was even good, and his sister-in-law was loyal to a fault and had taken Grace under her wing.

He knew Grace was extremely hardworking and responsible. Especially for someone who looked so young. She managed being a single mother and running Chalmers's office like a pro. They worked very well together. She was able to keep up with him, and in many ways he felt like she surpassed him. She knew all the patients by first name and things about them even he didn't. And hell, if they all didn't dote over Grace. They were all charmed by her.

Tonight, the ideas she'd proposed for the office had been impressive. And he thought that would have been the highlight of his night. But it hadn't. He actually found himself wanting to move on to personal topics. Like where Christopher's father was. And he'd already determined that wherever the man was, he was most assuredly an ass. The next thing he wanted to know was why she and Christopher had been locked out of their apartment, why they'd had nowhere to go. That made him angry. He'd thought about that day at the park every morning when Grace walked into the office, a smile on her gorgeous face and a sheen in her eyes that made him uncomfortable because it was so obviously a sign of gratitude. Sure, he knew she was grateful for his part in saving them from the accident, but this was something else. Grace needed this job, this break, desperately.

Grace stopped abruptly. "This is it," she whispered.

Evan looked down into her face. Her eyes glittered but her hands were clasped tightly together as she stared through the floor-to-ceiling window of what seemed to be an art gallery. The main lights were off, but small picture lighting glowed in the dark space, highlighting canvases.

"What's this?"

She didn't bother turning around, just stared through the window, her back to him. "The art gallery Holly was talking about. Somehow she managed to get me an appointment with them." The reverence in her soft voice pulled and tugged at him, until he was forced to feel. Again, *feeling*, that thing he'd managed to avoid for a long, long time, was rearing its ugly head inside him until he was forced to care. He needed to say something, ask something.

"I'd like to see your work." Not that. *God, not that.* Why had he just asked to see her art? That was…personal. That implied interest. And crap, but when she turned around, green eyes wide and glistening, did he realize that he was interested. Very. This other side to her intrigued him. A part of him wanted to be. And hell, if that wasn't going to send him up shit's creek with Grace holding all the paddles.

She gave him a slight nod and a little smile that again forced him to feel. Or maybe nudged him in the gut. "I'm going to go back to my apartment and bring my portfolio and whatever other pieces I can fit in my car. I haven't had a chance yet; it's such a long drive."

"Toronto's not that far. Even though it does feel like we're thousands of miles away from civilization."

He shut his eyes with a defeated sigh as the sound of her laughter enticed him. "Well, when you don't drive on highways it takes a lot longer," she said softly.

Evan shoved his hands in his pockets. She was still staring through the gallery window. Dusk had given way to the night, and the town was quiet. The faint rumble of thunder could be heard in the distance, reminding him of how muchs he used to enjoy spring storms out in the country. He hadn't thought of that in years. Or how many times he, Quinn, and Jake would get hell from their mother for not having enough common sense to not climb trees when there was lightening. But that brief period in time was so fleeting, all before things in their home grew tense.

He looked down at Grace, and for the first time didn't begrudge his upbringing. Because at the end of the day, after the shit had finally hit the fan and all the ugly secrets came pouring out, he was left with two brothers he'd die for, two sisters-in-law, and a nephew and a niece. He had family. But Grace was on her own, trying to raise a little boy and make something of herself. No one had her back. Sometimes, the way she or Christopher looked at him made him think he could have their backs, if he were a different man. "How the hell do you get back to Toronto if you don't take the highway?"

She shot him a gorgeous half-smile. "Ever heard of taking the scenic route?"

He shook his head. "I don't even know what that means."

She laughed and he found himself smiling. "You should try it sometimes. Cows. Horses. Country markets."

"Sounds like hell."

"If you think that's bad, you should try it with a four-year-old, alpha-male-in-training who feels the need to give driving directions from his car seat."

For some reason, driving with Grace and Chris and stopping at one of these country markets sounded… interesting. He remembered their accident. Grace had been on the on-ramp to the highway. Which meant…"So why don't you just take the fast way then?"

Her smile dipped and she turned her gaze from him. "I

haven't since the crash."

That admission hung there, weighty in everything that it meant. Neither of them had brought up the accident since her arrival with the muffin basket. They'd shared something profound, as strangers, and now neither of them could speak about it. She'd admitted something personal, a weakness, and she'd let him in. And hell, it bothered the crap out of him to think that she was embarrassed and afraid.

"You know that accident wasn't your fault."

She nodded, rubbing her upper arms as though she were cold. "It doesn't take away from the irrational fear. The kind that keeps you up at night, doing a second-by-second replay."

He clenched his jaw, his fists, in an attempt to reign in the emotion that pumped through him. They were both haunted by the memories of that day. "Grace—"

She tilted her chin upward. "Looks like rain. We should probably head back to your car." She attempted to walk past him, but he reached out to grab her arm. Her skin was cold under the palm of his hand, and she wasn't looking at him.

"Grace—"

"I should get Chris. I don't want to keep Holly up later than she has to be."

He held up his keys. "Drive my car."

"What?"

"Let's go. On the highway. I'll be with you." He didn't know what the hell came over him. But it bothered him. He didn't want her to be afraid of anything.

"I can't," she whispered, tugging her arm from his grasp.

"You can. Do you trust me?"

She paused. A long pause. Then she tilted her head to the side, her eyes narrowing on him. He straightened his shoulders. "That was meant to be a rhetorical question."

She smiled, almost laughing, and he found himself doing the same.

"Okay. I'll do it."

He pulled his keys out of his pocket and gave them to her. He wasn't going to acknowledge the pride he felt for her as she took the keys. Raindrops started falling and he grabbed her hand and they ran down the street to his car. His car was parked under one of the old-fashioned lampposts, and he opened the driver's side for her. He jogged over to the passenger's side, wet from the rain that increased intensity. The inside of the car was warm, and the only sound was the rain as it beat hard against the roof and windows. Grace was staring straight ahead, anxiety stiffening all of her features.

So he shouldn't be noticing how the rain had plastered the pale blue sundress to her body. Or that he had the insane urge to drag down the thin strap of her dress with his teeth, until there was nothing to hold it up. He wanted to kiss Grace, taste her lips and then…dammit. He should be offering Grace some sort of encouragement or diving advice instead of thinking like a redneck Neanderthal.

"It might be less intimidating if your car were a POS like mine," she mumbled while fumbling with the ignition.

"Don't worry about the car. That's what insurance is for."

She managed a little laugh.

He gave her a few pointers and instructions on some of the features of his car, so she would be more confident. She listened, taking a few deep breaths, and again, he struggled to focus on getting Grace to drive and not the impressive cleavage that was highlighted with each deep breath.

The engine purred, and she turned to him, her fingers gripping gearshift between them. The fear in her eyes propelled him to place his hand over hers. Her hand jumped beneath his. "You can do this," he said, his voice sounding hoarse to his ears. She gave him a nod and stared straight ahead.

And then in a split second, she'd pulled the key out of the ignition, slipped her hand from his, and practically jumped out of the car. Evan swore under his breath, and before she could get far, he met her outside. Rain poured down, and he grasped her shoulders. She was crying.

"Grace," he said, willing the odd lump in his throat to go down. For some reason, her tears didn't make him want to run the other way. They made him want to stay. And fix things for her. That should have been his first warning to pull back.

She squeezed her eyes shut and leaned her head back against the car, rain mingling with her tears. "I thought I could. I thought I could get all the memories of that day out of my head. But being in the car with you…Evan. It just brought me too close. I don't want to go back and conquer anything. I can't do it. I'm sorry."

He felt helpless for a second as he watched the torture play across her delicate features. But he wasn't a helpless kind of man. He didn't sit around and watch people suffer. He didn't know what the hell he was feeling, what he was thinking, except that he needed Grace to feel safe.

And he wanted to feel her against him, where he knew he could keep her safe.

He gently pried her hands off her face, holding her wrists. "You don't owe me an apology."

Her gaze leveled on his, green eyes bright and intense and filled with so much emotion that it slammed into him. "I owe you *everything*."

He didn't want that. He didn't want her gratitude. He wanted everything *but* her gratitude right now…and if that wasn't about to complicate the hell out of everything. All the promises he made not to get involved… He let go of her wrists and braced his hands on the car, on either side of her head, taking a step closer, feeling the shiver of awareness that ran through her.

Maybe he could convince himself that this was his civic duty. Good Samaritan stuff and all that other crap that was involved when a person lived in a small town like Red River. He was more than willing to sacrifice himself and offer up the best thing he could offer for easing any kind of pain.

He just wanted to make her feel better.

He leaned down and gently kissed the soft flesh beneath her earlobe. She clutched his biceps and let out the sexiest sound that had every single reason why he and Grace couldn't happen flying out the window. He trailed kisses along her wet skin until he reached her gorgeous, soft mouth.

Grace tasted like dessert, the sweetest he'd ever had.

She opened her mouth for him, and he deepened the kiss. When she tugged on the front of his shirt he stopped thinking with his head. He cupped the nape of her neck with one hand and hauled her against him. Rain soaked them, but all he could feel was Grace's body plastered to his, all soft curves and delicious woman.

"Evan, woo-hoo!"

Evan ignored the sound, a subconscious alarm going off somewhere in his mind that some kind of mental anguish was imminent. But answering to the person calling his name would mean extracting his mouth from Grace's, and he didn't plan on doing that anytime soon.

"Evan! Woo-hoo!"

Evan swore, and Grace let out a soft, sexy-as-hell little whimper against his lips. He looked up for a moment, turned his head in the direction of that voice, and spotted the damn raincoat in the distance. Jacobs. Then he looked back down at the woman in his arms. An infinitely better sight.

Never one to take a hint, Eunice called out again. "Evan Manning, is that you?"

"No," he yelled, over his shoulder. "It's not."

Then he lowered his head and kissed Grace like a starving man, who could only be filled by what she offered him.

# Chapter Nine

Evan squinted, tilting his glass so he could peer inside carefully. Dammit. Not an ounce of vodka left between the ice cubes. He let out a sigh, placing it back on the table with a *thud* a little too loud to be polite and looked around. No one had noticed. Then again, it was Eunice Jacobs's wedding, not a black-tie event. Could anyone hear a thing above the sound of that wretched conga line anyway?

Family. They filled the entire circular table he was seated at. His brothers appeared ridiculously happy, bordering on the idiotic in his opinion. And their wives, lovely of course, but again, a little on the nauseatingly happy side. Not that he begrudged them their happiness. Hell, no one was more deserving than them. Even their kids were happy: little Michael was sound asleep in his stroller beside their table, and Ella and Chris were rounding the corner in the conga line.

"Evan, why do you look like you're going to hurl?"

He scowled in the general direction of his brother, Jake.

"Everybody move back. Evan's had five martinis in the last two hours—"

"I did not. I was just wondering how I end up attending a wedding with you people almost every year?" Actually, he was wondering where the hell Grace had disappeared to now. All night she'd been avoiding him. And he could bet it was because of their hot-as-hell kiss last night. He hadn't been able to get enough of her. That was a problem. The only reason he'd broken off the kiss was because it had finally occurred to him they were on a public street, and the things he wanted to do with Grace weren't exactly acceptable in public. But when he finally managed to pull away, the emotion in her eyes had rattled him. He had told himself that he only wanted to comfort her, but he was a lying bastard. Because comfort didn't extend to spending the night in bed with Grace—which was exactly what he'd wanted to do.

But of course he'd pulled away, even though it had taken more self-control than he knew he possessed. Her lips had been swollen, her eyes filled with passion, and it had taken her a moment to regain her balance. She was sexy as hell. And off-limits.

He didn't know what they were going to do about that problem.

"Maybe the next wedding we attend will be yours," his sister-in-law Holly said with a wink.

He let out a choked cough. "Don't think so, Holly."

Dinner was winding down, and the newlyweds had already finished their first dance—a lively flamenco that had everyone on their feet clapping when it was over. He looked across the flower-and-candle-filled table at his brothers and their wives. It amazed him how perfect they seemed for one another. Like they fit together. The kind of stuff you saw in movies. The kind of relationships that he never really thought existed.

"You know, I think they make a sweet couple," Claire said, and everyone at their table turned to stare at her. His pretty sister-in-law's cheeks turned red. "I know Eunice drove me crazy when we were planning the flower arrangements for the wedding at my shop, but they really are cute together. And despite their age, they're getting married, ready to start again. I've got to admire that. It's like they knew that being alone was so much worse than taking the risk to love someone," she said, linking her fingers through Jake's. His brother mumbled something but leaned forward to give Claire a kiss on the temple.

"So I just found out some interesting news," Quinn said, leaning back in his chair. Of course, when his eldest brother spoke, everyone listened. Quinn had that quiet authority and the man knew how to use it. "Apparently, our boy Ev here was seen inhaling Grace's face last night in Port Ryan."

A series of gasps and snickers made their way around the table. Dammit.

Holly punched Quinn, "Why didn't you tell me?"

"I just found out—news was traveling down the conga line." He laughed, holding up his hands.

"What are you doing participating in a conga line, anyway?" Evan muttered.

"Hey. My little girl asks me to dance? I dance."

"I really like Grace," Claire said, more to Holly than to him, as though he hadn't even spoken. Grace fit in. Almost as though she'd known them all for years. Other than blushing a few times when Chris would make some too-loud comments on all the food, she and his sisters-in-law had talked nonstop.

Holly nodded. "Me, too, she's perfect," she whispered to Claire, who nodded. Evan wasn't about to ask, *Perfect for what?* because that would mean he was entertaining whatever future plans they were making for his life.

"Thanks, Quinn. Just what I needed tonight," Evan said lifting his glass in salute.

Quinn's smiled grew wider. "Not a problem, man. It's great having you back in Red River. And I'm happy you're having such a good time here. According to the second rumor in the conga line I heard something about some…how was it worded again? Ah yes, sexy-time shenanigans going on in one of the change rooms at Sally's store."

Again more gasps and snickers. He needed to find his partner in these escapades, and he needed to find her before someone brought up the blasted chickens.

He stood, pushing the chair with the back of his knees. "It's been a pleasure, guys." Evan stuffed his hands in his pockets and looked from his sisters-in-law to Grace, who was now standing under one of the lit trees on the edge of the woods.

"Later," Evan said, not waiting for a smartass comment from any of them.

His eyes were on Grace, who was slowly walking farther into the trees. Claire and her team of florists had done an amazing job, turning the old apple orchard into something that looked like it was straight out of a fairy tale. In May, all the apple trees blossomed with spectacular, showy white flowers. And then Claire's crew had strung tiny, twinkling white lights through the branches. The effect was spectacular, especially now that the sky had darkened to a deep, inky indigo.

He weaved his way around the round tables, his eyes on Grace. He was stopped a few times by different patients he'd seen during the week. They told him how much better they were feeling or updated him on their condition.

His mind was on Grace, not wanting her to get away. Finally, he was able to make his way over to her. The live band struck up an old jazz favorite, and the hum of the music wafted through the trees, Grace clearly in his sight. His eyes traveled the curvy length of her body, and he noted with a slight smile that she had taken off her heels and was holding them in her right hand.

. . .

Grace sensed Evan approaching. She slowly turned to look at him, her breath catching in a flurry of attraction. His thick, dark hair was clean-cut but mussed up enough to make her ache to run her fingers through it. Wide shoulders filled out his dark suit, and the crisp, white shirt highlighted the sun-kissed skin.

She couldn't get last night out of her head. Evan had kissed her like she was the only woman in the world. His lips had been hot and demanding, his body hard and protective as she'd stood in his arms...and held on for dear life. Need had consumed her. Desire had filled her until he'd ended it, he the only one of them having enough common sense to remember they were on a public street.

Evan gave her a half smile as he stood in front of her. "Hi," he said in a deliciously deep voice. The look in his eyes told her last night was still very much on his mind.

She attempted a smile up at him, suddenly wishing she hadn't taken off her heels. "Hi." She sighed deeply, the words on her tongue not the ones she really wanted to say. Maybe it was the wedding, maybe it was the martinis and champagne his family had been forcing down her throat, but what she wanted was to pretend that they were together. But then she remembered that all this was fleeting. He was leaving, and she was determined to stay and start a new life. He wasn't a man who wanted a family, a wife. He didn't want father-hood, and she needed to recite that over and over again... especially when he looked good enough to eat.

She toyed with the straps on her sandals as she held them in her hands. "I'm sorry I flaked out last night with the whole driving thing."

"Don't be. You weren't ready, that's all," he whispered in a voice that made her toes curl into the ground. "You shouldn't be so hard on yourself. You'll get there. But, the consolation prize was pretty good," he said, giving her a slow, sexy grin. "C'mon," he said, holding out his hand.

"Evan, I don't think any of this is a good idea," she whis-pered. She could hear the low chatter of guests, and the slow, romantic music from the band encircled them out here in the privacy under the trees. She glanced over at Christopher, who was busy dancing with Ella.

"A dance, Grace." His deep voice was deliciously gruff, his blue eyes shadowed under the twinkling lights. Her mouth went dry. Last night, she'd had a taste of Evan, and she couldn't forget. The feel of his hard body against hers, the taste of his mouth, the pressure of his lips...the uncon-trollable desire she'd felt when he kissed her as though she were the only thing in the world that existed and he wasn't ever going to let go. She was falling for him, and he would be the third man in her life to leave her. She couldn't do that. Not this time, because she had Christopher to think about.

"Grace."

Her heart kicked into a gear it had never operated at with anyone else, and she knew what her answer was going to be. She couldn't say no.

"Just a dance," he murmured, reaching out for her. The instant his large, warm hand enveloped hers, she knew she wouldn't be able to refuse him.

"I think we should talk first," she whispered in a futile attempt to gain some control. "About the chicken debacle," she blurted out in an attempt to distract him.

His laugh sounded strangled, but he didn't miss a beat. Instead he looked even sexier, with his eyes twinkling. "Don't think about the chickens. They're being battered and fried —"

"That's awful." She laughed.

"Come here, Grace," he said, gently pulling her to him.

She drew a shallow breath, enough that the scent of him sent a shiver of awareness through her.

Evan's hand curled around hers, pulled her close, and she slowly relaxed against his tall, strong body. She inhaled the tantalizing scent of his cologne, of him. The gentle sway of his body against hers was lulling her softly into a place that still had dreams. There was something about being in his arms that seemed so reassuring and at the same time completely electrifying. His chest was hard and powerful under her cheek, and his arms were solid and strong.

"I don't know what we're doing, Evan," she whispered.

"Neither do I, sweetheart," he said gruffly.

*Sweetheart. Sweetheart. Sweetheart.* The endearment he'd whispered that day. She looked down at his hand, and a wave of recognition stole through her. Memories of the accident flashed through her psyche. Memories that would only surface at night, while she slept and had no control over her subconscious. *He's fine. He's going to be okay. I'm getting you both out. I'm going to get you out of here, sweetheart.* She tried to breathe. Her eyes burned with tears as she stared up at Evan. In unison they both stopped dancing. He stood still, his expression almost unreadable except for the slight frown.

She reached out for his right arm, her eyes not leaving his. She took his strong hand in hers, slowly turning it over, and then she looked down. At the angry red marks that had transformed his otherwise perfect flesh. She had seen them, working with him every day, but she'd always looked away quickly. But now…she couldn't run from this man anymore, or the feelings she'd developed for him. She paused for a second, taking a deep breath before unbuttoning his cuff. And he let her. He stood there, and she slowly rolled up his shirtsleeve and revealed the forearm that was still strong, still powerful, but battered and scarred. She shook her head, and her body trembled as the truth swam through her with a velocity that she wasn't prepared for. The truth, the damage to his perfect body was entirely overwhelming.

"Say, 'Everything is going to be fine sweetheart,'" she whispered.

He clenched his jaw, his eyes not leaving hers. Familiar. "Pardon?"

She tried to breathe against the heaviness in her chest. "Please. Say, 'Sweetheart, everything is going to be fine.'"

He swallowed, his face hard, his eyes filled with anguish. "Sweetheart, everything is going to be fine," he whispered roughly. She closed her eyes against the onslaught of memories. Her forehead fell against his chest. Flashes of blue eyes, of hands, of whispered reassurances played across her mind as she fought the memories, of the reality. The memory of his scream and the orange blaze stole the remaining breath from her.

Her voice trailed off, and she covered her face, unable to fully grasp the enormity of everything that had just happened. She felt Evan's strong, warm hands slowly grasp hers, taking them off her face. "I don't know how I can ever—"

"Don't," he whispered roughly, his lips hovering over hers for a second until finally covering her mouth. Evan Manning's lips on hers started a fire within that melted her, made her knees weak and her breath stop.

"Dr. Nevan, Mommmmm!"

Half a second later, Christopher and Ella plowed into them, almost knocking them over. Evan squeezed his eyes shut for a moment and then looked down, slowly extricating himself from her. A cool breeze billowed between them.

"It's Evan, not *Nevan*," Ella said with authority.

• • •

"Oh well, I think I'm allowed to call him Nevan," Christopher said. It took all of Evan's self-control to concentrate on their conversation. His mind was moving so quickly, the reality of Grace and how attracted he was to her filling him. He knew he was attracted. He knew she was beautiful. But what he hadn't counted on was the emotional level she hit him with.

"Well, Ella, Christopher and I sort of have a special agreement. He can call me Nevan, because I think it's a pretty cool name," Evan said, ruffling his niece's brown hair, which was in complete disarray. He winked at Christopher who was beaming up at him.

"Hey, guys," Holly said walking up to them. Evan tore his gaze from Christopher to look at his brothers, sisters-in-law. All of them that had chosen this particular moment to come up to them.

Grace mumbled some sort of greeting as everyone started chatting within seconds, he could tell she was still shaken. His family talked around Evan and Grace, not even noticing that they had just walked in on something.

"You know, we should probably get going," Quinn said a moment later.

"What, the night's still young? Evan here looks like he's ready to party. How 'bout we all have a round of drinks?" Jake said.

He normally would have laughed. And joined in Jake's banter. He would have insulted his brother and then drank with him.

"I'm exhausted," Claire said, shooting her husband a frown. "And so is Michael." Her obvious attempt at supporting their need to depart was interrupted by Michael, who decided it would be fun to run through everyone's legs—acting the exact opposite of tired. Ella and Christopher thought it was hilarious and egged him on to run faster.

"Well, I'm wiped, too. I can't stand for another minute," Holly said, leaning on Quinn. His brother wrapped his arm around his wife and nodded.

"Yeah, let's get going." He motioned for Ella. *Finally*

they began saying good-bye to each other. Minutes later, after ridiculously long farewells by people who saw each other almost every day were exchanged, Evan, Grace, and Christopher were left standing in the orchard.

"Mom, can we go now, too?" Christopher asked, tugging on Grace's arm.

Grace opened her mouth, looking from Evan to Christopher.

"I'll take you home," Evan said, before Grace had a chance to walk away from him again, and before he remembered that he wasn't a family man.

# Chapter Ten

The drive to the coach house was filled with Christopher's hilarious chatter about the wedding. Evan was grateful for Christopher's ability to speak a mile a minute, because it enabled him to check his emotions. Whatever that meant. Because he wasn't supposed to have messy emotions. And he wasn't supposed to go near women with children. Now, not only was he near, he had just experienced one of the most emotional moments of his life—with a virtual stranger, a woman who was undeniably beautiful but deserved so much more than he was willing to offer. But the connection he felt with her was hard to ignore. As was his growing attraction.

"And my favorite part was that *cake!*" Christopher said, barreling through the door he held open once they arrived home. "Did you have some? Mrs. Jacobs said she ordered that extra chocolate layer just for the kids. Ella liked it, too. And then Michael came over and smashed his whole hand in the side of the cake. It was so funny, and then his dad came over and pulled him off the cake. And then Ella said that her Uncle Jake wasn't really mad, and that Michael wasn't going to get in trouble because he's just a toddler," he rambled on, taking off his shoes.

"Chris, it's really late. Why don't you run upstairs and get your pajamas on, okay? Don't forget to brush your teeth—especially after all that cake," Grace said with a smile as she hung up her sweater.

"Okay." Halfway up the stairs, Christopher turned to look at him. "Good night, Dr. Nevan."

Evan smiled and then tried not to frown as a jolt of something hit him in the gut. Maybe it was the reality that he was starting to mean something to this kid. And that was something Grace had warned him about. "You don't have to call me Doctor."

"So I can just call you Nevan?"

"Yeah," he said hoarsely. "Just call me Evan. Or Nevan."

"I'm glad you're here," Christopher blurted. And then, as though he were embarrassed, he smiled and ran up the stairs.

"I'm sorry for acting weird back at the wedding." She stood there in her pink dress, her hands clasped tightly together, her large eyes filled with that vulnerability he sensed from her growing more intense. Grace wasn't a woman who would play by his rules. She was someone who'd obviously been deeply hurt before and was trying to start over. To make a mess of her emotions would be cruel. She needed a man who would be by her side forever. She needed a man who could offer her stability and family. None of the things he wanted out of life.

"You didn't," he said.

"Evan, this is all like a dream for me, for Chris. You

rescued us from that car accident and then you rescued us again. This entire place," she paused, lifting up her arms, "is like a castle to us. I have never had anyone show me the kindness you have."

He closed the distance between them, pushing all his reasons for not getting involved with Grace aside. Holding her or comforting her wasn't getting involved. He was just being…a good friend. He told himself that it was normal for his lips to brush the top of her head, to inhale her familiar, sweet scent. It was normal for his lips to slowly move down. But when her face tilted up to his, it was anything *but* normal to capture her mouth beneath his.

To hell with that. Normal was highly overrated.

He gently clasped the nape of her neck, her thick hair soft and silky beneath the palms of his hands. And then he pressed his lips to the soft flesh below her earlobe, slowly kissing his way down impossibly smooth skin. He pulled her closer, nudging her head up until he could capture her lips between his.

"Evan," she whispered against his mouth, her hands on his arms.

He slipped his arms around her as Grace sank against him, her soft moan of pleasure filling him with a need to explore every inch, to know every sound, every taste of her.

"Mom, I'm ready for you to tuck me in," Christopher called from the top of the stairs.

• • •

"Omigod," Grace whispered, pulling back from him abruptly.

Evan Manning knew how to kiss. She blinked, and he

held onto her arms, like he knew that she hadn't regained her composure.

"I'll be right up," she called out. Her voice sounded strained to her own ears. She smoothed her hair and offered a quick, "I'll be right back," to Evan. She gave him a glance before taking the stairs two at a time. Good God, he looked even sexier than before. His shirt was slightly rumpled, his hair disheveled, and his eyes…had the unmistakable gleam of desire in them. All it took was the slightest touch, and she was melting into his arms, all thoughts of self-preservation long gone. Oh, Evan was getting more difficult to ignore and so were all the reasons for not getting involved with him. Every time she brought up his family or Red River, he didn't even attempt to hide his enthusiasm to get back to the city. He'd break her heart; he'd break Chris's heart.

She tucked Christopher in as quickly as she could, grateful that exhaustion was finally setting in on him and his questions were at a minimum.

"I had lots of fun, Mom. I really like it here. I miss my room at home, but I really like Red River. And I like Ella even though she's a girl. Most of all I like Doctor Nevan. I mean, Nevan. He's really cool. And I never get to hang around guys, you know?"

She nodded, trying to listen to her son and battle her own feelings for Dr. Nevan. She tried to hide her insecurity, her feelings of inadequacy behind her smile. The reality was that after Chris's father walked out on them, she hadn't been with anyone else. And the thought of Christopher facing heartache if another man came into their lives stopped her from letting anyone close to them. But seeing how happy he was with Evan made her wonder if she'd been too

protective…

She smiled softly, ruffling his hair. "I'm glad you made friends already and that you like Evan so much. I really like it here, too." She frowned, touching his cheeks. "Are you feeling all right? You seem kind of warm, honey."

He yawned. "I'm okay, just tired. Do you think we can go back home soon just to get Charlie?"

She nodded. She had promised him they would go back and get his favorite dinosaur. It had been the first stuffed animal she'd given him, and he'd taken to him right away, sleeping with him every night. Somehow in the rush to pack, they'd forgotten him. And she needed all her portfolio thanks to Holly.

"Let's plan to go next weekend, okay? I want to get my art stuff, too." Christopher's eyes finally drifted shut, and Grace didn't move for a few moments. She knew Evan was waiting for her downstairs.

Her eyes wandered over him as she tread softly down the stairs. He shrugged out of his suit jacket, tossing it on one of the armchairs. She tried not to let her admiration for his allure, the masculine beauty that he possessed, distract her. His broad shoulders were clearly defined in the crisp white shirt, the lean lines of his torso, his long legs.

He smiled as she reentered the room. "He's asleep?"

"Hopefully," she said with a forced laugh. She joined him at the patio doors where he was standing. Moonlight hit the river, illuminating the choppy waves.

"Nice view from here," he said. His hands were tucked into his pant pockets, and his strong profile was serious.

"I love looking out this window. Every morning before Chris gets up, I have my coffee at the breakfast bar, work on my To-Do list, and then stare at the water. It looks different every day. Is it bad for me to admit out loud that I secretly hope no one moves in for a long time?"

He chuckled. Evan had a delicious laugh. Low and throaty and the corners of his eyes crinkled slightly. "Nope. Wouldn't blame you a bit."

"Have you been inside the main house?" She'd been tempted many times to peek through the windows of that grand home but was too scared one of the Mannings might drive up and think she was nosy. Now that she knew Holly so well, maybe she'd just ask her.

He shook his head. "No, but I can get the key if you want to look at it one day. My brothers are excellent at what they do, and so's Holly. I'm pretty sure the place is spectacular."

"Kind of hard to imagine something even nicer than this house," she whispered.

He turned to face her, close enough that if she moved forward one step she'd be back in his arms. "Grace?"

"Yes?" She was a coward. Maybe she should do what cowards do and run. Who was she kidding? There was no running from this man.

He reached out to cup her face, and she held her breath. His thumb trailed her lower lip gently, and a small sound escaped her mouth. Good Lord, the man had barely touched her, and she was already gone. His lips were smooth and soft, his hands on the nape of her neck, tangling in her hair. The minute she parted her lips, his tongue sought entry, exploring. He tasted of champagne and want. She had never been kissed like this. She and Brian had been so young, and it had been so many years ago. But Evan Manning was a man. He knew how to kiss her, how to consume all her thoughts and senses until she couldn't form a thought that wasn't about him. His strong hands left her hair and traveled down the side of her body, lighting a fire, a hope, a need.

"Mom!"

They both stopped. "Omigod," she whispered against his mouth. She felt as though she'd just been ejected from an airplane and was now freefalling.

"Mom!" This time the panic in her son's voice registered, and her mind cleared.

She ran toward the stairs. Evan followed her as she took the stairs two at a time. He stood in the doorway while she walked over to turn on the light on the nightstand. Christopher was sitting up in bed, his face red.

• • •

"I don't feel well," he said as tears fell from his eyes. Evan's gut constricted, and he walked over to the bed where Grace was already sitting beside him.

"What hurts, buddy?" Evan said, feeling his forehead, even though he already knew he had a fever.

"My throat," he said in a small voice.

"I think it's his ears," Grace said softly, smoothing the damp hair that clung to Christopher's forehead. "Every time he gets an ear infection, his throat hurts, but his ears never do," she said, a frown of worry creasing her forehead. "He had so many ear infections when he started preschool that we were referred to a specialist," Grace said.

Evan clenched his jaw tightly. "Who?"

Grace named the doctor, and he had no idea who he was. He knew plenty of good specialists. "I've got my medical bag in my car. Why don't I run out and get it, and then I can have a look at your ears, okay Chris?"

Christopher nodded and lay back down.

"In the meantime, go ahead and give him some ibuprofen," Evan said, halfway out the room. He bounded out the house, grabbing his car keys along the way. A minute later he was back, feeling something tighten in his chest when he heard Christopher crying.

"Please, Mommy," Chris was saying when he walked into the room.

"It's late at night. We'll go tomorrow if you're feeling better okay?"

Christopher shook his head, looking miserable. Evan sat beside him, and Grace quickly scooted onto the other side of Chris in bed. "Something I can help with?" Evan asked, opening his bag.

Grace sighed. But Christopher spoke up before he could, "I want to go home, because I want Charlie," he said in a little voice, his face crinkling down into the saddest frown. Evan's heart constricted. He looked over at Grace.

"Charlie is his stuffed dinosaur, and we forgot him," she said in a small voice.

"Mom promised we'd get him, but I want him now. He helps me feel better," he said, furiously wiping the tears that fell down his face. Evan felt the boy's mounting frustration. He calmly pulled out his otoscope. "I'm going to have a quick look at your ears, okay, Chris?" Evan said, helping him into a sitting position as he looked into his left ear. He wanted to keep him talking. "So, Charlie is really important to you?"

Christopher nodded dramatically, and Evan switched ears. "Let me have a look inside your mouth, too, okay?"

"The specialist talked about possibly putting tubes in his ears, but then the ear infections stopped."

"He definitely has an ear infection now," Evan said, straightening. He ruffled Christopher's hair and smiled down at him.

"I'll head out to the pharmacy and have an antibiotic prescription filled. Any allergies to medication?"

Grace shook her head.

"Dr. Nevan?"

Evan paused for a second while gathering his instruments. "Yes?"

"Can you get the kind that tastes like banana?"

Evan smiled, snapping the clasp on the bag. "Definitely."

"What about Charlie?" Christopher whispered to Grace.

"As soon as you're better, we'll go get him, okay?"

Christopher shook his head, frowning. It was the first time Evan had seen him less than agreeable. His heart tugged as the little boy's chin trembled.

"Is your place downtown?" Evan asked Grace.

Grace cleared her throat but didn't look at him. "A little to the east of the city, but I really don't think it's a good idea—"

"I can pick up the penicillin on the way, and Chris can sleep in the car. Then he can sleep in his own bed tonight, with Charlie." Christopher was now grinning at him, causing him to practically start with surprise at the emotion that ran through him because he'd made Chris…happy. *He'd* done that. He looked over at Grace who was sitting straight and looking very pale.

Chris coughed for a few moments and then asked again, "Please, Mom?"

Grace visibly caved the moment her son started coughing. "Okay," she whispered finally.

"Great, we can take your car if that's easier—"

"Mom never drives on the highway. It'll take two weeks to get home," Chris said, pulling the covers off, then tugging them back on. "I'm cold," he said with a shiver, even though his face was red. Christopher should be resting, but then again, if they indulged him tonight, then big deal. The ibuprofen would kick in, and he'd probably fall asleep on the car ride.

Grace scrambled off the side of the bed, straightening out her dress, which was now beyond wrinkled.

"Mom said taking the long way is good for us and allows us to appreciate nature."

"Okay, Chris, I don't think Evan needs to hear all my different driving-route philosophies."

She stood in the doorway for a moment, and Evan was caught off guard by how young and vulnerable she looked.

"I can help Chris get ready while you change. We'll meet you out front," Evan said.

"Evan, are you sure? You don't have to do this."

"I know. I want to."

She gave him a small nod and then walked out of the room.

"You tired, buddy?" he asked Christopher as he helped him out of bed.

"A little. But it's kind of fun to be going out past my bedtime." He shot him a grin. Evan smiled back at him effortlessly. "Am I allowed to go out in my pajamas?"

Evan nodded, looking at the kid's Spider-Man pants and shirt. "It's late at night, and you're sick." He hesitated a moment and then extended his palm. His chest constricted when Christopher's warm, small hand readily accepted his. They waited for Grace at the front door, Christopher not as chatty as his usual self.

Minutes later he was helping Christopher into the backseat of the car while Grace locked the front door and followed them out.

He didn't know why, but this whole thing, helping Grace with Chris...the wedding...the kiss...this should not be something he liked. This should be making him want to run in the opposite direction. Except there was no place he'd rather be right now than with this woman and her son. He'd chalk it up to temporary insanity, get the dinosaur, and then pray things went back to normal inside his head before he got in too deep.

• • •

Fat, round drops of rain smattered against the windshield, the only sound besides the even purring of Evan's BMW as they pulled into the parking lot of the pharmacy. Almost midnight, it was virtually deserted. Christopher had fallen asleep almost immediately, and she and Evan had talked quietly about the little things. It had felt so good to have an adult's company. A man's company. Evan's.

"I'll run in and get the medication," he said. A second later, she watched as he ran across the dark parking lot, the rain pelleting relentlessly. Grace turned in her seat to look at Christopher, a strange sense of comfort and insecurity at the same time entering her. How many times had she struggled, after sleepless nights and doctor's appointments? And now, Evan was here, capable, strong, and so tender with her son?

When Christopher had begged them to go, she saw the look on Evan's handsome face. The strong lines in his perfect face had softened, and her heart had thumped painfully as she watched. And had foolishly imagined what it would be like to be Evan's wife. She leaned her head back against the headrest and closed her eyes. *Count to three, Grace and then remember why this will never be your reality.* Evan had made it clear he was moving on to bigger and better things when his time at Chalmers's clinic was over. And let's face it, she was never anyone's idea of bigger or better. Evan would be bored with her in five seconds flat. Sure, she looked better now, and for some reason they shared a mutual attraction. But that must have come from the fact that it'd been a while since he'd been with anyone, and the last woman had been a witch. She was safe for Evan. But then he'd leave and never look back. A single mom in a small town would never be enough for him.

She jumped as the door opened, Evan sliding into the driver's seat. He shook the rain off his hair and then looked at her, pulling out a bag. She bit her lower lip as emotion hit her, when he looked at her, shrugging as he handed her a few coloring books and a pack of markers.

"While I was waiting for the prescription, I thought maybe Christopher would like these. I remember he likes coloring, but…" He shrugged, his voice gruff as it trailed off. Grace blinked rapidly, putting the coloring book and crayons back into the bag.

Grace managed a wobbly smile. "He loves coloring, and he's obsessed with cars."

Evan gave her a brief nod, and moments later, they were on their way to the on-ramp of the highway. He drove in silence, the only question about which exit to take. Exhaustion was slowly taking over, but she knew she wouldn't fall asleep in the car. Ever since the accident, she had never been able to relax in a car, let alone relax enough to sleep.

Grace sat tense in her seat as rain pummeled against the windshield, the rain making the dark road difficult to see. He reached across and captured her hand in his, its strength reassuring as it rested on the armrest between them. Evan's competent, if not fast, driving reassured her, but she knew she wouldn't feel completely calm until they were pulling into the parking lot of their apartment building. She breathed a sigh of relief as he exited the highway, and she quietly directed him to their apartment building. Moments later, he pulled into a parking spot of the small building. Christopher stirred in his seat, mumbling when the car stopped.

"Christopher, honey. We're home, okay?" she said. He gave them a sleepy smile and then just shut his eyes again.

"I'll get him," Evan said softly, opening the car door.

She followed, grabbing the bag from the pharmacy and her purse. By the time she'd climbed outside, Evan had Christopher in his arms. They hurried to the front door, Christopher's head resting trustingly on Evan's shoulder.

"It's just up two flights of stairs," she said quietly as she led the way across the empty lobby and to the stairwell. The building didn't have an elevator, and she'd never really minded until now. Evan looked around, and she wondered what he was thinking.

Once inside the small two-bedroom apartment, she purposely turned on the dim hallway lamp instead of the brighter overhead lights. It was silly, but she didn't want to reveal how little they had to Evan. "Christopher's room is down here," she said once they'd placed their jackets on the hooks beside the front door. Evan was still in his suit pants and shirt. He followed her silently down the hall, Christopher resting comfortably in his arms.

She flicked on the car-shaped bedside lamp and turned down Christopher's quilt. Evan slowly lowered the little boy onto the bed. "I want to give him a dose of penicillin before he goes to sleep for the night," Evan whispered.

"You got the banana one?" Chris asked, sitting up.

Evan smiled, nodding as he poured the medication into the plastic measuring cup. He held it to Chris's lips gently, waiting for him to swallow it all.

"That was great, thanks," he said, flopping back onto his pillows. "It feels good to be home. This is Charlie." He handed Evan his green dinosaur.

Evan turned it around, examining it. "This is a really cool dinosaur. I can see why you needed to come back and get him."

"Should I put that medication in the fridge?" Grace asked.

Evan nodded, giving it to her.

"I'll be right back, Chris," she said. "Do you want some water?"

Christopher nodded. Evan sat on the edge of the bed beside Christopher and tucked him in. Once she had a glass of water filled, Grace approached Chris's room quietly, not sure whether or not he was still awake.

"Thanks for driving us home—Mom never would have brought me here tonight. I know the real reason my mom doesn't drive on the highway anymore. I'm not supposed to know this, but sometimes I accidentally hear things I'm not supposed to. You know, like when adults are having a conversation, and I'm playing or something and then I just hear things they're talking about?"

Grace clasped her hand over her mouth. She wanted to die. How did he know all this stuff? If she walked in now, she would be humiliated. No, maybe she'd just linger in the hallway and die of mortification alone, in the dark.

"I heard Mom talking to her friend, and she was saying that she knows she's afraid to drive after the accident. And that she'll work on finding the courage to drive again. Of course Mom would never tell me this. She tries to pretend she's a superhero sometimes." Chris shook his head.

Tears pricked her eyes, and her sweaty hands cupped the glass of water.

"I met a superhero once," Chris said with a big yawn. Evan was smiling at him, and Grace's heart squeezed at the man's patience for her chattering son. The ibuprofen must have kicked in, because Chris's face was looking less flushed. Evan reached out to smooth his hair, and tears pricked the back of her eyes.

"So where did you meet this superhero?"

"Well, when I was little, like three and a half years old, my mom was driving, and this giant truck crashed into us. And we were stuck in the car, and I was crying—because I was little and sometimes little kids do that. I couldn't see anything; the car was filled with so much smoke. So then, all of a sudden a superhero came in and rescued us before we got all burned up. It was you! I didn't know it then, though. But my mom said it wasn't a superhero." Christopher sat up, as though he were about to confide something huge.

Grace held her breath.

"Who did she say it was?"

"She said an angel rescued us."

# Chapter Eleven

Grace stood in the doorway, feeling completely exposed. She didn't dare make a sound. Evan's back was to her, and she didn't know whether or not he knew she stood there. Christopher's eyes finally shut as he settled into his pillow. Maybe it wasn't so bad, what Chris had revealed. Maybe Evan wouldn't believe him; he'd just think it was a four-year-old's overzealous imagination.

"He looks a little better," she whispered softly, still standing in the door, not wanting to approach Evan. He jumped slightly when she spoke and turned around to look at her. For the briefest, sweetest second, she saw the man that she could fall hopelessly in love with. But then he turned from her and stood, and all the reasons that could never happen infiltrated her mind again. She tread softly across the room and placed the glass of water on Christopher's nightstand. She leaned down to kiss him lightly on the forehead, pleased that his skin felt much cooler. They walked out into the darkened corridor.

"Fever's down. When he wakes up, we can give him his next dose of penicillin," he whispered. He wasn't standing close to her, but the hallway felt small and consumed by him.

Grace nodded.

"I've got my hospital bag with a change of clothes in the car. I'm going to go grab that. I'll sleep on the couch," he said in a low voice.

"Are you sure? It won't be very comfortable. I don't mind taking it."

"Grace, I'm not going to have you sleeping on the couch. I'll be fine. Be right back." He walked down the hallway, capable and sure. She wondered if Chris had scared him off. Who wouldn't be scared? A single, broke woman with a kid. Chris had now painted her as a woman who had hang-ups and believed in angels.

She didn't move until she heard the front door close. Evan was spending the night. She quickly pulled out a spare blanket and pillow and walked into the living room. She frowned at the way the room looked. It was a clean but no-frills space. She decided not to turn on the big overhead light, opting to just let the lamp on the entryway table cast a dim glow in the room.

The front door opened, followed by the clicking of the lock, and then Evan appeared in the doorway. She gingerly placed the pillow and blanket on the couch. Somehow it felt odd to fluff the pillow and spread out the blanket for him.

"Thanks," he said.

"No problem. Um, thank you for helping with Christopher and the medication—"

"No need to thank me," he said, his blue eyes steady on hers. She swallowed and gave a small nod. Why was everything so awkward? Oh, yeah, maybe it had something to do with the kiss. Or kisses.

"Do you want anything? Water…?" Her voice trailed off as he shook his head. He'd turned his back and was unfolding the blanket. She wrapped her arms around herself, exhaustion finally setting in. His hair was disheveled and wet from the rain. He was standing in her living room, looking irresistibly male with five-o'clock shadow and a damp shirt that clung to him, reminding her how strong and powerful he'd felt when she'd been in his arms.

"Good night," she said softly walking out of the room, feeling stupid. The only time a man had been in their home, and she'd never felt more alone.

"Grace?"

She stopped and turned around. "Yes?"

"Where is Chris's father?"

• • •

He didn't know why he should care. Well, yes, he did know, so that he could want her and have her without worrying that he was going after another man's woman.

"Long story," she whispered, looking young and vulnerable. Chris's words about Grace thinking he was an angel replayed over and over in his mind. And he didn't know what the bigger problem was: that she still believed in angels or that she believed *he* was an angel. Yeah. An angel who wanted to be the CEO of private plastic-surgery clinics instead of staying in his hometown with his family.

"How about a glass of wine? I find they go well with long stories."

She gave him a wobbly smile. "I think that's a great idea.

I believe I have my emergency bottle over the fridge cupboard."

He walked with her to the small kitchen. "Emergency, eh?"

"You know those days where your nerves are shattered and you're too tired to think?"

"Hell, yes. I've had days like that. So my question elevates this to emergency status then?"

She took two wineglasses out of the cupboard. "Uh, I'd say it's pretty close. Can you get that bottle down for me?"

"Sure." Seconds later he was filling their glasses.

"Thank you," Grace said, taking a sip of wine. "Do you want to go into the other room?"

Evan nodded. "Sounds good."

Grace settled on the couch beside him, a healthy dose of space between them. "So, um, Chris's father. Where do I start?" She tried smoothing her hair down and he fought the urge to lean across the couch and tangle his fingers in it and kiss her until neither of them remembered why they weren't a good idea.

He waited for her to start speaking. Instead she tucked a leg under herself. Then looked into her wineglass. Then shifted again. "Grace?"

She lifted her eyebrows innocently.

"You stalling?"

"You bet."

He laughed.

"So…Christopher's father…" She took a deep breath and he counted to ten. He wasn't going to rush her. "I didn't really have a lot of friends in high school. I didn't really have time for that. I was always working after school to help my mother with the bills. Brian and I had a few classes together and clicked. His mom was a single mother as well, and he knew exactly everything I'd been through. I didn't have to be embarrassed around him. He and his mom had even slept at the same shelter as we had." She shot him a cheery smile that he knew was fake as hell. And it made him hurt for her.

"He was always saying how he was going to make something of himself, how one day he'd make enough money to help his mom, and he'd raise a family. We shared all our dreams and in my first year of art school, I became pregnant with Chris. Neither of us could ask our parents for financial help. I dropped out of school, worked full time…and so did he. Supposedly." Her smile was gone and he picked up the bottle of wine and refilled her glass, when he realized she was reaching for it. This Brian guy was shaping up to be a world-class ass.

"He totally had me fooled. We shared the same values, goals, beliefs. Every Saturday morning we'd work at the youth shelter on Gerrard. Hey, you must know it. It's so close to Toronto General."

Evan swallowed past the lump of inadequacy in his throat. "I, uh, am usually in a rush when I get to work, and after I'm too tired to notice anything."

She didn't say anything for a second and then that light was back in her eyes. "Of course. No, I mean, you're a doctor; of course you must be so busy. You even took the time to save us!"

Evan realized that look, that admiring light in her eyes. And somewhere along the way, she had gotten the impression that he was a stand-up guy. Hell, maybe she looked at his brothers and thought he was the same as them. And she couldn't have been further from the truth. He shifted on the couch.

"So he was happy about the baby?"

She nodded, rubbing her hands on the front of her jeans. "He was. There was no way he'd walk out on us; I was sure of that. His own father had, just like mine, so he was determined to be a good dad."

She took a long sip of wine before speaking again. "He'd come home every night and when we'd lie in bed at night, he'd rest his head against my stomach and talk to Christopher. He'd tell him how much he loved him, how special he was, and all the things he wanted to teach him."

*Jeezus.* Who was this guy? She stopped speaking abruptly and stood. "Grace," he whispered, surprised by how hoarse his voice sounded.

She shook her head, her back still to him. "It's okay. I'm fine. I always cry at this point, when I remember."

"Because he's gone?"

"No. Because this is where my mother dies. And then he walked out a month later. We were months behind on our rent, and he confessed to not having a job. He actually left every day before I did and pretended to work. I had nothing. Nothing, Evan. And then Chris was born two months after that." She hastily swiped her eyes, and he realized she was crying.

He cursed softly. He leaned forward, bracing his forearms on his legs. This was more than he expected. She couldn't have been more than twenty-five or twenty-six. Had she actually done all this alone at such a young age? With no one? He'd sensed she had an inner strength. But he hadn't expected this. Or the undeniable respect for her that pummeled through him.

"Yeah, I said something along those lines, too." She squeezed her eyes shut for a moment. "Pretty pathetic right? I mean, how could I have fallen for that act? I should have known."

"How could you know something like that? He's an ass. He had responsibilities. To you and his son."

She shot him a sad look. "I know."

"Does he keep in touch?"

She shook her head. "Nope. I guess all that professed love for the baby inside my stomach didn't translate to any sort of obligation or sense of duty on his part."

The jerk probably wasn't even paying a dime. "So that was it? He just left you two alone?"

She nodded. "Yup. I was twenty-one and scared out of my mind."

"I'm sorry," he whispered roughly.

"He was the first and only. And I promised myself that if I ever got involved with a man again, he would be a real man. One who had principles, one who would put us first."

Shit. He kept his head down and forced his features to remain calm. But he was getting in way too deep and he saw no way out. Her douche-bag ex had been her first and only. He didn't want to know that. He didn't want to acknowledge what that meant. Even though he suspected it before, it was now confirmed that whatever he and Grace had between them was more than just lust for her. What the hell was he going to do? How was he better than Brian? He should leave them now.

He wished he could be the man she needed. But he couldn't. He had never thought about a life beyond his career.

Even when he'd been with Alex for those years, they were just two surgeons existing together. They had never been in love. Neither asked the other for anything, and one always understood when the other had to cancel plans. There were no hurt feelings to try and manage or kids to raise.

Her hands wrapped around her waist, and she looked at him squarely, bravely revealing the rest of herself. "But I can't complain, you know? I had a wonderful mother. My father wasn't great; he walked out on us when I was six, and maybe that's what bothered me so much about Brian. I should have known. I should have seen the signs that we weren't number one in his life. Just like my father." She shook her head and stared up at the ceiling.

"What about your father?"

"The few memories I have of him aren't really the best. He was miserable. I remember hiding when he'd come home from school. I'd sit in my closet with a flashlight and draw. I'd draw happy people. Families at parks. I'd draw anything that wasn't my life. I vowed when I found that I was pregnant with Christopher that there would not be one day that my child would ever question whether or not he was loved. Because that doesn't go away, Evan. It stays with a person. As much as I've grown up, I carry it with me.

"I will never forget the day my father walked out that front door. He never protected me, never laughed with me or took me to the park. It shouldn't have hurt so much when he left. But it did. I used to think that parents had to love their children; it was a given, right? But that wasn't true, not when parents see their children as the cause of their misery. He turned his back on us."

"Grace, I'm sorry." Evan's throat was clogged with

emotion as he imagined Grace as a quiet little girl watching her father leave, feeling not good enough. But this, that feeling of not being good enough for a parent he could relate to. It was something he'd never spoken to anyone about.

"Don't be. In the end, I was left with a wonderful mother. Even though we didn't have much, I knew that I was important to her. I knew if my mom held my hand, that wherever she led me, we'd be okay. One night before Christmas, she led me into the shelter on Gerrard. I didn't know it right then, but it was going to be our home for a few months. I still love that place, because everyone was so kind to us.

"When my mom died, I felt like I lost the only person in the world I could truly count on. One night, I was lying here on the couch, Chris on my chest, finally getting him to sleep after a night of crying. And I was zoned. Just watching TV and wishing my mom were still here with me. And I just wanted to hold her hand again, to see where she would take me. I would never again hold the hand that gave me comfort."

Evan couldn't breathe and couldn't utter a word as she looked up at the ceiling, visibly struggling for control. "But then Chris, my little one-year-old, reached out and locked hands with mine, and I knew he was my new reason for living. So that day that you saved us, Evan, I will never ever be able to repay you."

This time, when the tears poured from her eyes, he walked across the room, leaving his doubts, his goddamn stupid beliefs on the couch and gathered her into his arms. This time, he let himself feel everything he'd shut himself off from so long ago.

• • •

Grace was aware that something was different. Something had changed. When he gently lowered his head, the moonlight that streamed through the window exposed the unmistakable tenderness in his eyes, the determination on his face. She still couldn't speak. She'd told him everything. Her body brushed against the hard, strong lines of his as he stood in front of her.

"Grace," he murmured. She squeezed her eyes shut at the emotion in that rough whisper. At the tenderness as his hands cupped her face. They were warm, large, and so gentle. This was Evan. But when his lips made their way to slowly, achingly kiss and drink the wetness on her face, she let her head fall against his hard chest. His hands roughly moved to the back of her head, holding her hair.

"I'm sorry, sweetheart. I'm sorry." The tenderness in his deep voice, in the hands that held her to him, was new to her. Grace held her breath when his eyes went from hers to her lips. She sucked in her breath when his head ducked close to hers, a mere inch from her mouth.

"Evan," she breathed.

"God, I want you," he rasped before his mouth captured hers. He destroyed every ounce of fear, every wall she'd ever put up, as his firm lips claimed hers. His hands plunged into her hair, and his hard body locked against hers until her entire reality was Evan. She opened her lips, her mouth welcoming his exploration. Evan kissed her like no one man ever had. He consumed, possessed and cherished her until her knees gave out. He scooped her up in his arms and seconds later they were in her bedroom, locking the door behind them.

His hands moved from her head and roamed her body, the palms of his hands grazing the side of her breasts, the heat from his skin warming her through the cotton of her shirt. She sighed against his mouth when his fingers grasped the edge of her shirt and pulled it over her head, letting it fall to the ground.

She pulled at his shirt, and seconds later it was gone. She reveled in the sight of his body, lean muscles and tanned skin. And then her eyes lingered on his arm. She took his arm in her hands, cradling it, the uneven, rough texture of the scars a poignant reminder of what he'd done. "I just want to say…" She paused for a moment, tears clogging her throat, but she wanted him to hear, before she lost herself in Evan. She trailed the outline of his biceps, up his hot flesh, delighting in the ripple of muscle beneath her palms, until her hands reached the nape of his neck. "Thank you—"

"Don't," he grated. "Don't say thank you to me." He wouldn't let her speak, his mouth already on hers again, this time demanding and powerful, until her knees wobbled. His hands moved restlessly down her body until they settled on her hips, his hands tugging the sides of her jeans until he pulled them down. His eyes were on her, everywhere, as she stepped out of them. His stubble pricked at her skin as his mouth wandered down her neck and shoulders, pausing for a moment at the swelling flesh above her bra and then lower, until he knelt down, kissing the soft flesh below her navel.

She sucked in her breath as his hair tickled her skin, and his lips opened onto her flesh, above the line of her underwear. She grasped his strong shoulders to steady herself as he slipped them down her thighs until they fell to her feet. His hands held her hips, and he traced the scar that encompassed half her abdomen. She tried to cover it. She knew how ugly it was. This wasn't what she wanted him to see. Her body had changed after Chris.

But before insecurity could spoil the moment, Evan gently, firmly pushed her hands away and traced small kisses along the entire line. And then he stood, cupping her face in his hands, backing them onto the bed. And then he was there, everywhere.

She let herself go, welcoming his touch, his love. His blue eyes, stormy, filled with the same burning passion that she was feeling, met hers. "God, I want you, Grace." Evan's mouth swooped down to claim hers as his body covered hers. He claimed her insecurities, her heartache, and her loneliness.

. . .

Evan lay on his back, staring at the ceiling of Grace's apartment. It was early morning, and not a sound other than the distant hum of city traffic could be heard. He glanced over at Grace. Her dark hair was tousled around her shoulders and splayed across the white pillow. Her fine features were relaxed, and she looked young and beautiful. And he had no idea what the hell he was going to do now.

He'd woken during the night to give Christopher another dose of medication. The memory of Chris saying that Grace had told him an angel had saved them replayed in his mind. It reminded him of when he had been a kid and had an unwavering faith and belief in good and right. But

Grace still believed in angels and miracles, and he believed in science and facts. She'd had more faith than he ever had. And then the image of them trapped in that car haunted him, because now he knew them. They weren't strangers anymore. They were so much more. He'd just spent the best night of his life with Grace. All he knew was that right now, he was going to enjoy this. His time with her and her son.

Grace stirred beside him, turning her face into the pillow and stretching under the covers. He leaned over, placing a kiss on her bare shoulder. One eye opened and then she smiled at him until he was grinning at her. "Good morning, Ronald," he whispered.

She gasped and then punched him in the stomach. "How did you know about that?"

He caught her fist, laughing, before rolling over and pinning her under him. "I heard you mumbling in front of the mirror. For the record, you have way better hair. Much sexier," he said, leaning forward and giving her a kiss.

"Evan, what time is it? I should go check on Christopher," she said.

He kissed her shoulder. "I already did. He's still sleeping soundly."

"Thank you," she whispered.

He frowned, reaching for his phone on the nightstand as it vibrated, a text message coming through. He braced himself on his forearms, not wanting to leave Grace. It was from his brother, Quinn. For chrissakes, he could bet ten bucks he knew exactly what this text was going to be about. He had no idea how his poor sister-in-law was dealing with Quinn. He was usually the levelheaded, calm guy, but ever since Holly had become pregnant, he'd been a wreck.

"Hold on a sec," he said to Grace. "My brother, Quinn."

*Holly's having contractions for the last forty minutes. This is it.*

Evan cursed under his breath. This was the fifth time his brother had contacted him this week.

"Is something wrong?" Grace asked.

"No, Quinn just thinks Holly's going into labor. Every. Day." He typed in a message. *Relax. This is not it. Call me if they're ten minutes apart.* There. That should do it. "Holly's been having Braxton Hicks contractions on and off, but he keeps thinking it's the real deal. They always go away in an hour."

His phone vibrated again. *They are twelve minutes. Then fifteen. Then Thirteen.*

Evan pounded the keypad. *That's not ten.*

He didn't bother putting his phone away until Quinn texted him again. And seconds later his brother's reply came in. *FU.*

"I love your family." She laughed, reading over his shoulder.

"They're one of a kind."

"I think I'm going to take a quick shower before Chris gets up," she said, taking all the covers in the process.

"Thanks, Grace. I don't need covers."

She smiled but didn't look him in the eye as she tossed him the blanket, keeping the sheet for herself and almost falling in the process. She was across the room in a second.

"Grace?"

She turned around to look at him and that vulnerability he'd seen far too often from her was back on her face. Because of him. "You okay?"

She nodded and then ducked out of the room.

He cursed quietly as he fumbled for his jeans. He knew last night meant a lot for her. And it had for him as well. She wasn't just any woman. Now he just needed to figure out how they'd be able to walk away from each other in a few weeks, without any hurt.

He looked around the small bedroom. Now that it was daytime, the signs of wear and tear were more evident. It was obvious there wasn't any extra money for the usual items that would make a home more comfortable. The space held only a closet, two simple nightstands, and a black chair in the corner. The place was neat and tidy, and there wasn't a speck of dirt anywhere. It wasn't poverty level, but it wasn't a typical middle-class home either.

He turned around, breath trapped in his lungs as he noticed the wall at the far end of the room. Early morning sunlight spilled through the window, highlighting the dozens of photographs of Christopher and Grace in simple, black frames. He slowly walked over to get a closer look, jamming his hands into the pockets of his jeans. He studied Chris as a newborn, baby, and toddler. Christopher's smile he recognized—it was Grace's. Moisture stung the backs of his eyes and blurred his vision as he viewed every picture. Since when did he want to know everything about a woman?

# Chapter Twelve

Grace was in the kitchen, unaware that he was standing in the doorway. He took in the sight of her, her hair damp and falling into dark waves down her back. Her pink T-shirt and dark jeans clung to curves that he'd spent the night admiring with his hands and mouth. As if she sensed his presence she turned, her mouth opening when their eyes made contact.

"Hey," she said, picking up the coffee carafe and filling it with water. Evan walked to stand in the doorway to the tiny kitchen. A small white table was pushed against the wall, and two white chairs sat at opposite ends. The kitchen was a cheery yellow, and a few potted herbs were on the windowsill above the small sink.

"Hi."

"Coffee?" she asked, taking the lid off a canister.

"Please," he said.

"At least it stopped raining," she said, before spooning in the appropriate amount of coffee grinds. "Christopher seems to be sleeping well," she said. The politeness was killing him. He knew she was scared. Once they had gotten out of bed, reality had hit. He wanted to offer her reassurances, to say that she didn't need to worry, that he'd be around for the long haul, but he couldn't.

She walked over to a cupboard beside the coffeemaker, and took down two mugs.

The coffee percolating sounded loud as they stood there.

She poured the steaming liquid into the cups and handed him one. "Thanks," he said his fingers brushing against hers, startled by how cold she was.

"I don't have any milk or anything fresh. But you take your coffee black don't you?"

"You're still here," Christopher said, appearing in the doorway. He gave Evan a sleepy smile that tugged at all his heartstrings. "Don't worry, Dr. Nevan, I get sick all the time. No need to be scared," he said leaning back to look at Evan.

He noticed Christopher's eyes were almost completely identical to Grace's. Except Chris's were filled with unabashed happiness, innocence, and adoration. "I'm just really happy to see you."

"Good morning, sweetie," Grace said in a soft, if not shaky voice. She leaned down to give him a kiss on the head. "Are you hungry?"

Christopher nodded eagerly.

"Okay, have a seat, and I'll see what I can come up with." She peered into the refrigerator.

"Do we have bacon and eggs?" Christopher sat down across from Evan.

Evan smiled. "That's my favorite, too."

"Sorry, love. How about toast with jam?" Grace asked,

hands on her hips. Evan ripped his eyes from the sight of her breasts straining against the pink T-shirt. There was a child in the room, and he needed to keep his thoughts PG.

Christopher nodded. "Okay, that sounds good. Can we stay here today? Maybe I can play in my room for a while?"

Grace looked over at Evan. Evan nodded. "That's fine by me. It's probably a good idea for you to have an easy day, Chris."

"Maybe I'll run out to the grocery store, pick up a few fresh things, and I can make you some chicken soup?" She was busy toasting the bread that she'd retrieved from the freezer.

"My mom makes the best chicken soup ever," Christopher said, leaning forward at the table.

Evan smiled as Grace placed a plate of toast in front of Christopher. "Here you go. I found some juice boxes, too," she said, placing one in front of him. "Evan, can I get you something?"

"I'm not much of a breakfast eater," he said taking a sip of coffee.

"Do you wanna play with me? I have loads of stuff in my room," Christopher said, in between giant mouthfuls of toast.

"Sure, buddy."

"Evan, you don't have to—"

"I want to. Really." It was the least he could do. Because somehow, someway, he was going to have to leave them in a few weeks. But right now he was here, and this kid saw something in him, so he'd go with it. Then he'd figure out how the hell he was going to leave…

"Um, okay, you can play, and I'll head out to the store.

Chris, you make sure you listen to Evan, okay?" Grace said softly, leaning against the counter.

Christopher nodded, slurping the last of the juice from the box. Evan watched her, even though she was looking into her mug.

"Evan, I wanted to ask you if you have some room in your trunk…would you mind if I brought back some of my art work?" The hesitation in her voice and the vulnerability in her eyes tugged at him.

"Of course, that's fine," he said. "But I get to see them first, don't I?" She stood in the doorway.

"Sure."

"Is this for the gallery Holly mentioned?"

Her flush deepened, and she nodded. "It's actually a really long shot. But I'm meeting with them next Monday."

"You deserve a chance to get your work out there," he said gruffly.

She turned away from him, but not before he caught the sheen in her eyes. "Thank you," she whispered. It hit him then, how much he hated seeing her quiet and unsure. She was vulnerable, everything stripped down, and she was fragile. Like she doubted him. Like she regretted last night.

"So I'll get ready and head out to the store." She looked awkwardly between him and Christopher. A thought occurred to him, and he quickly told Christopher he'd be right back. He walked to the front door where Grace was gathering her purse and getting her jacket from the hall closet.

He cleared his throat. "Let me give you some money for the groceries."

She shook her head. "I have money. I know this doesn't look like much, and—"

"Don't do that. I'm not going to have you buying me food," he whispered, very aware that Chris was in the other room. He smiled. "Besides, I eat a lot." He pulled out more than enough bills and then opened her hand, pressing it in. "Don't argue."

"I know you come from a long line of extremely stubborn men, so I'm not going to argue. Thank you," she said, placing the bills in her wallet. "Good-bye, Chris, I'll be back soon," she called out, not making eye contact with Evan.

"Bye, Mom!"

"We'll be fine," Evan said opening the door for her. She gave him a tiny nod and walked out. Evan let out a deep breath. He headed back into the kitchen as Christopher stood from the table.

"Okay, so ready to show me around your room?" Christopher nodded and tore past him, down the hallway. Evan chuckled, happy that he seemed to be doing so much better than last night.

He followed Christopher and stood on the threshold and stopped breathing as the room, in the light of day was fully visible. He hadn't seen any of this last night. And it was so obvious, standing here, on the edge of what had to be something almost magical, that Christopher was her entire world.

Each wall was adorned with a different mural. All brilliant, vivid colors. There was a wall with trains, one with dinosaurs, one with jungle animals, and one with superheroes. It was a stark contrast to the scarcity of rest of the apartment. This room was filled to the brim. There was a Thomas the Tank Engine table with train tracks and at least a dozen brightly colored miniature trains. Blue-and-white-striped buckets lined one wall, and they were stuffed with cars and dinosaur figurines. A blue bookcase lined another wall, packed with board books and an array of photographs. Under the large window, there was a small bench, and Evan's heart constricted when he saw the small plastic insect containers. He'd had those as a child. He'd loved catching caterpillars and spiders.

He walked over to the bed and gingerly sat on the edge while Christopher yanked some toys from the boxes. He ran his hands over the quilted Spider-Man pillowcases. His throat ached, and he found it hard to breathe. He'd never been so blown away by a woman. Every time he thought he'd figured her out, there were more layers. More depth.

It was obvious that whatever extra money Grace had earned went to her son. The rest of the apartment was spartan.

"Your room is really cool, Chris," Evan said. Christopher stood up with a handful of trains and nodded.

"Thanks. My mom did all this for me. I still remember when she painted it all. I was little, like three. It took her months. And she'd even let me paint some, even though I wasn't really good at painting back then," he said smiling.

Evan loved the sound of his voice, the expressions that played across his face as he spoke about Grace. But why? Why did this kid's nonstop talking not irritate him?

"Do you want to play trains? I know they're kind of babyish now, like none of my friends at school still play with this stuff, but I know my mom spent a lot of money on this. She gets me stuff. Even if we're going out for something she needs, she'll get me stuff instead. I feel kind of bad sometimes, but she says that's what moms are for. Do you like her?"

Evan felt as though someone had just punched him in the gut. Grace's son was a running fountain of information, and he switched topics of conversation faster than Evan could keep up with. Evan cleared his throat, attempting to find his voice again. Did he want a dad? Was this a four-year-old's attempt at setting up his mother?

"Yes, I do like your mother," he said gruffly. Christopher let out a big sigh and flopped down on the bed beside him, trains tumbling around him.

"She's a nice lady. And she works really hard. And she's an artist you know? She's got this whole other room that I'm not allowed to go into unless she's there. But she's really good at it. And she loves me more than anything. Remember the accident?"

He nodded, not saying a word.

"She stayed with me in the hospital, and I was there for almost two months. She got me treats, and she slept in my room every night. Do you need a nice lady in your life, Dr. Nevan?"

This kid was killing him. It was like he was taking a dull knife to his heart and carving it. *Do you need a nice lady in your life, Dr. Nevan?* He ran his hands through his hair roughly. "I hadn't really thought about it, Chris."

The little boy frowned. "Oh, well when you do think about it, you should think about my mom."

Chris had the makings of a fine salesman. "Okay, I'll keep that in mind. But, we should probably start playing." He picked up a red train. "Your mom is pretty cool," Evan forced from his throat.

Christopher beamed at him. "We're going to have a

great time today."

• • •

Hours later, Evan was sprawled on his back on Christopher's floor. Chris hadn't stopped talking for more than two minutes, and that was only because he'd needed a washroom break. But then he would say something incredibly clever, and Evan would find himself so damn proud of him. And he had a funny sense of humor, too. He was cheerful and full of energy.

Evan finished reading the last line of the spider book Christopher had selected and looked over at him. He was sleeping, sprawled out on his bed, one arm flung over his dinosaur and the other on Evan's leg. Evan slowly placed his hand on the bed and tucked him so he was snug under his Spider-Man sheets. Grace had checked in when she came home from grocery shopping, but Christopher had begged for more time with Evan. Of course he'd agreed, and Grace said she'd use that time to cook. And Evan had sent a quick text to Quinn checking on Holly, and sure enough, she was just fine and not having any more contractions.

Evan quietly closed the door behind him, giving Chris one last glance before he went in search of Grace.

He walked down the short corridor and swung open the door to the small studio, thinking she was in there. He walked in and stood in the center of the room and slowly turned around, his mouth dropping open as he stared at hundreds of paintings, sketches, drawings.

He walked over to the lone sketching table, frowning slightly as one caught his attention. Evan stilled as he spotted a leather portfolio with Christopher's name scrawled across the front in Grace's handwriting. He gingerly flipped the book open, and emotion slammed him in the gut. It was a sketch of a man with an infant. The man was bare-chested, cradling his son against his body.

The man had no face. And he refused to acknowledge the thoughts crawling through his mind about who that man should be. Or who he wanted that man to be.

His hand shook as he flipped the sketch over to look at the next one. There were more of the same, of Christopher as he grew. He saw him through the various stages of infancy, and in all of them, the faceless man was holding him. There was adoration in Christopher's eyes as he looked at the man that would be his father with a pure, undiluted love that made the hair on the back of Evan's neck slowly stand. He continued to flip through the pages, unable to look away, wanting more. There was one of Christopher holding the man's hand, standing at the water's edge tossing in rocks. Grace had sketched all of these. And they were all this faceless man, as though he'd actually been there and lived these moments.

This is what Grace wanted for her son. She wanted him to have a father. He kept flipping through the book, unable to stop. There were a series of sketches with Christopher and an older woman; Grace's mother. Evan knew she had never met her grandson. He took a deep breath, frowning at how ragged it was. Like there was something in his chest, and he knew it had nothing to do with his lungs.

He was holding in his hands everything he'd been running from his entire life. Emotion, love, vulnerability. Grace epitomized all those things. She had a depth to her that scared the shit out of him. He squeezed his eyes shut and rolled his shoulders, attempting to downplay the memories of the accident that night. Now they weren't just strangers. Holly's mantra, the "everything happens for a reason" line that she dished out for every major and not so major event that happened in any of their lives, gripped him. Hell, but if that didn't make him wonder. It had been him that night that pulled them out of the car. And if he hadn't...none of them would be here, together.

He couldn't remain indifferent. Being with Grace meant being real. And nothing about their arrangement was supposed to be real. Christopher wasn't supposed to get attached to him. But hell, he hadn't counted on the fact that he might become attached to Chris. And Grace...she was supposed to be his pretend wife. But he wanted her. For real.

"Evan?"

Grace's soft voice yanked him from his thoughts, and he turned around. She stood in the doorway, and the woman he'd thought beautiful the first time he met her was now a goddess. Her work, her passion, her dreams were poured into these paintings and sketches. She was brilliant. And he was so damn proud of her. And in awe of her. Because Grace, coming from a home with so little, had accomplished so much more than him in many ways. He didn't say a word as he battled with his conscience. He wanted her. "I didn't mean to invade your space. And I've never been into art, but even an idiot would know that your work is amazing. You're amazing."

Grace's gorgeous mouth dropped open. And he wanted to tell her how amazing she was, every day. But he knew that wouldn't happen. So he could settle for now. Today. He'd show her. With words, with his lips, his tongue, he'd show her all the ways in which he thought she was amazing.

Evan took the room in two strides, shut the door with one hand, and slipped the other into her hair. He caught her gasp with his mouth. He had the inexplicable need to taste the emotion, the woman who made him want to forget all about his goals, his priorities, his promises. He wanted Grace, in bed, out of bed, and in his mind.

He backed her up against the door, and she pressed her body against his, making the sexy sounds she'd made last night. His hands wandered down the soft curves of her body and then reached down to cup her sweet ass, lifting her until she wrapped her legs around him like she'd never let go.

"Where's Chris?" she whispered against his neck.

"Asleep."

"I'm not sleeping!" They both froze at the sound of Christopher's voice. Panic shot through him until he realized the voice was coming from the other side of the door. He slowly helped Grace stand.

"Nevan I told you not to go in my mom's art room! She doesn't like people touching her stuff!"

Grace slapped her hands over her mouth, and she almost doubled over laughing.

"Would it be really wrong if I swore quietly?" Evan asked.

Grace managed a smile. "Life with a kid."

"Hey, I thought we were eating soup!" Christopher yelled from the other side of the door.

Right. Life with kids. Something he'd never, ever contemplated.

Minutes later, the three of them were seated around the

table, eating the best damn soup Evan had ever tried. Chris had already inhaled his second bowl and was now peering out the kitchen window.

Evan leaned close to Grace. "So I guess it would be really crass if I wondered whether any of those chickens you rescued are now in this soup?"

Grace choked on the spoonful she'd just put in her mouth and then punched him in the arm.

"I hope we get a thunderstorm," Chris said, looking up at the window, rain pouring outside.

"You like thunder?" Evan asked, spooning another mouthful in.

"Love it. And lightning, too," he said, completely missing his mouth as a crash of thunder startled him.

They all laughed, and Grace wiped the soup spill with her napkin. "After you finish, Chris, I want you to get ready for bed, okay?"

"Aww. Do I have to?"

She nodded. "We're having a late dinner. And you're still sick even though you're feeling better, okay? Tomorrow morning we need to get an early start."

"Your mom's right. How about I read you a story before bed?" Evan asked, without even thinking twice. It seemed natural. Especially when Chris's face lit up and he grinned at him.

"Deal, Nevan," he said, wiping his mouth and running out of the room.

"Call me when you're done," Evan called after him. He looked over at Grace, who was idly pushing her spoon around in the bowl.

"You okay?" he asked leaning forward.

She lifted her green eyes to his. "It occurred to me that you know almost everything about me now, and I still don't feel like you've told me anything about yourself."

. . .

Grace finished the last of the dishes and wiped her hands on the dish towel, staring vacantly ahead as the rain trickled down the windowpane.

"I was going to offer to help clean up," Evan said, walking into the room. She spun around, surprised that he'd come in without her even hearing him.

"That's okay. You tucking in and reading Chris a story is help," she said, attempting a smile. But it was hard to smile casually. She had revealed so much of herself last night to Evan but he hadn't done the same. Every time she spoke of family he didn't respond. And then out of nowhere, the letterhead from Medcorp appeared in her mind. There was so much about him she didn't know.

But the little things she did know—the tenderness she saw when he was with Chris, in the faint lines around his blue eyes as he smiled at her son, the way it softened his features, the richness in his deep laugh when Christopher did something comical. And of course, the way he'd made love to her last night. That hadn't been something she had been prepared for. She hadn't let anyone come close to her since Brian. And when she'd been with Brian…it didn't compare with Evan.

And he'd seen her work. Her sketches. She knew her entire soul was revealed in her paintings, almost more than any words she'd ever said to him.

He walked over to stand beside her at the sink, looking out the window. "Quite the storm," he said, his deep voice loud in the tiny kitchen. The heat that emanated off his strong body was so foreign in this space. She wasn't used to sharing the kitchen with anyone other than herself and Chris. But he filled it up, all the emptiness and made her realize just how hollow things were before him.

"Talk to me," he whispered, tugging her over to him. She spread her hands against his chest, the strong beating of his heart thumping against her palms. She couldn't be drawn into the cocoon of security and safety he offered until she knew more.

"Last night complicated everything, and I don't want to make this a bigger deal than it needs to be…" She tore her eyes away from his serious gaze and stared at his shoulder instead. Much easier. "I mean, I know for you last night might not have meant anything—"

"Not true. It did mean something."

She nodded rapidly, feeling slightly like a bobblehead. "I should go pack up my art room."

"Grace." He captured her hand, his mouth pulled into a straight line.

"Before you tucked Chris into bed, I asked about you. Why it feels like you know everything about me and yet I know nothing about you?"

He leaned back against the counter, his features impassive. "That's not true. You probably know more about me than anyone except my family."

"That doesn't exactly reassure me."

He gave her one of his sexy half grins before wrapping her up into his arms. "I can spend all of tonight reassuring you," he whispered against her hair. She closed her eyes and wished it were that simple. If she hadn't learned from an early age that people she loved walked out on her, she might have been able to relax. But there was one thing different this time—Evan wasn't like her father or Brian. She had never had a connection with either of them like she did with Evan. No one had ever made her feel as safe as Evan, and yet that didn't make any sense at all. How could a man who hadn't really given any of himself, or made any promises, make her feel safe?

She knew deep down that Evan hadn't given his heart to her. But he had shown them more compassion and kindness than any man. He had won Christopher over, had become her son's real-life superhero. Maybe, somehow, he'd have a change of heart. Maybe he would see that a life in Red River, with them, could be good enough for him.

Somehow she was going to have to get through this next week and then the gala. She would keep her end of the deal. And she would allow herself this time with him. Even though she had just broken every promise she'd ever made to herself, she knew she had fallen in love with him. Hopelessly. She hugged him tighter, burying her face in the warmth of his neck, drinking in his scent, feeling his strength, and silently made wishes like a little girl.

"Grace," he whispered against the top of her head. His lips brushed against her hair, his voice sounding rough.

She squeezed her eyes shut and stayed still in the safety of his arms. "Tomorrow we'll have to leave super early to get Chris to school on time and then to the office. Next weekend is the hospital gala."

And then it would all be over. The fake fiancée. His

position at the clinic. He'd be back in Toronto. She waited for him to answer. To say that it would be okay, that they'd figure something out. Instead, he gently grasped a handful of her hair and pulled her head back and looked at her. The raw emotion in his eyes stole her breath, followed by his mouth on hers. He silenced all her worries as he kissed her, demanding and yet giving, lifting her onto the counter until all she could think about was spending the rest of the night in his arms.

# Chapter Thirteen

Grace tugged on Evan's arm. "Evan?"

He stopped before entering the ballroom and then pulled her into a discreet corner. She let her gaze roam over him one more time. She hadn't been able stop looking at him since he'd picked her up earlier tonight. Evan Manning in everyday clothing was already gorgeous. But in a tuxedo, he was devastating. He wore it confidently, as though he'd been born to wear one. She, on the other hand had tripped in her stilettos a few times while practicing around the house. Thankfully, she hadn't repeated that mistake tonight.

This last week had been the best of her life. Evan had come over for dinner every night and played with Chris and read him bedtime stories. After Chris went to bed, they'd sneak up to her room, lock the door, and spend the rest of the night in each other's arms. Evan had drawn out this whole other side to herself she didn't know she had. And then he'd tiptoe out of the house, early morning before Chris woke.

And every morning when she watched him drive away, she swore that she wasn't hopelessly in love with him.

Maybe she was fooling herself, and maybe she'd broken every promise she'd made to herself, but she was hoping, wishing, that Evan would be different. There were parts of himself that he still kept from her, but she convinced herself that in time he'd open up. He had to.

"What is it, Grace?"

She frowned, her eyes darting to the interior of the opulent ballroom. She could hear people laughing and talking, crystal clinking, and live music playing. "I'm scared I'm not going to fit in, and I'll ruin all of this for you—"

"Grace?"

She nodded.

Evan leaned down, cupped her face and kissed her until she opened her mouth and let her arms climb the length of his chest. He broke the kiss and stared down at her with eyes that held the promise that tonight wasn't going to end in the ballroom. "You could never embarrass me," he said, his voice gruff. "You're stunning, you're smart, and you're the only woman who has ever made me want to be better. There's no one else I'd want by my side tonight. You don't have to do anything but be yourself. Tonight is a formality and nothing more."

She opened her purse, wanting to fix her lipstick after that kiss, but Evan grabbed her Spider-Man notepad. She snatched it out of his hands. He had an adorable smirk on his face. She raised an eyebrow. "Yes?"

"I need you to add something to this list," he said in a low voice.

"I really don't need more things to add," she mumbled.

"Trust me, you do. You need to add me to your list."

She squinted at him as he leaned against the wall, all smiles and sexiness. "Pardon?"

He pointed to the sheet with "TO DO" written on top. "Add my name under that. Do, Evan Manning."

She choked out a laugh, and he grabbed her, his head at her neck, his warm laughter melting her. "Play your cards right, Evan and I'll be scratching that item off my list by one a.m."

A few heated minutes later, he held out his hand, and she grasped it, a tremor rippling through her as she realized the significance of the gesture.

She tore her eyes away from his blue ones and looked into the ballroom. It was a sea of silk and marble and silver and crystal. It was nothing she had ever been exposed to or even thought of. She glanced up at Evan, taking in his confidence, reveling in the power. She could do this for him.

. . .

Three hours later, dinner was over, and Grace was feeling like there was so much more to this evening than Evan had let her in on. The meal had been pleasant, the couples they'd been seated with polite but reserved. No one really spoke to her, so she'd eaten quietly. Evan had been attentive but very focused on what she assumed was him catching up with old colleagues.

She took another sip from her wine glass and scanned the crowd for Evan. He wasn't too difficult to spot, even in a group this large. Her stomach did that odd little flip that she had grown accustomed to since meeting him. His broad shoulders shook as he laughed at something an older man said. His profile was visible, his tanned skin contrasting beautifully to the vibrant white of his shirt. As he'd done many times these past few weeks, the man amazed her. He fit in here beautifully, as though he was born for this. And yet at home, in Red River with his brothers and family, in jeans and T-shirts, he looked equally comfortable.

"Evan Manning is a man who stands out in a crowd of hundreds, isn't he?"

She spun around in her heels to meet the owner of the smooth, cultured voice. A lovely, tall, dark-haired woman stood beside her. Her perfect features were impassive, her full lips the only indication that she wasn't exactly pleased. "I'm Alexandra. Evan's long-time girlfriend."

Grace stood a little taller, clutching her wineglass a little tighter. "*Ex*-girlfriend, you mean."

Alexandra's lips tightened. "We broke up because of a misunderstanding."

Grace tried her hardest not to be drawn into the cattiness. She truly hated this. Yet every jealous bone in her body ached for her to set this woman straight and hold her ground. And hold onto her man. The man who now looked nothing like the man she'd grown used to seeing the last few weeks. But the one who must seem very familiar to Alexandra.

"Your loss, my gain I guess."

"Evan must be dying to get out of Red River."

Grace's spine stiffened. "What makes you say that?"

Alexandra scoffed. "Please. That town? It's wasted on a man like Evan. What's he supposed to do there? Run a two-bit family practice?"

"He has family there—" *And me and my little boy.*

"Trust me. That's not enough for him. I know Evan in a professional sense, and I understand him. I know what makes him tick; I know what gets him off. He's a man who needs to be the best, at the top of his game. He thrives on competition. And there is no competition in Red River," she whispered, leaning down into her personal space. Grace was about to tell her she too knew what got Evan off, when she felt his hand at the small of her back.

"Hi, ladies." At the sound of Evan's deep voice, Grace turned to face him, trying not to look as though she'd just been railroaded by Doctor Evil.

She shifted from one uncomfortable, stiletto-clad foot to the other as Evan's ex-girlfriend simpered on and on about how good he looked. Alexandra had thrown herself on Evan like a dirty towel.

Grace took a long sip of champagne and eyed the woman over the rim of the crystal glass. She was as tall as Evan, with a perfect porcelain complexion, dark hair, and even darker eyes. She was lithe, with sculpted shoulders and arms and wearing a short sequined dress that showed a hell of a lot of leg. And in Grace's uneducated opinion, the woman had had one too many Botox injections.

She frowned when Alexandra touched his arm and laughed at something he said. She had no idea *what* the woman could be laughing at since Evan hadn't even said anything funny. She glanced around the room and tried to ignore the jealousy that wound its way through her body.

Alexandra turned to Grace all of a sudden. "And what's your specialty, Grace?"

Grace frowned at her. What was she talking about?

"Grace isn't a doctor," Evan interjected. Grace tried not to smile as Evan's hand intertwined with hers.

Alexandra's red lips formed a perfect *O* as she continued to stare at her.

"Though my son does call me, Dr. Mom," Grace said before she could stop herself. At the pure disgust that Alexandra showed her, a flush made its way up her neck and over her cheeks. The woman was a complete snot. She raised her glass to her lips again and this time took a longer swallow of champagne. If Holly and Claire had been here, they would have had her back.

"What *is* that on your hand?"

Grace sucked in her squeal of mortification. She had forgotten about the damn bandage. Of course, this morning in her rush to get everything done, she'd cut herself while slicing an apple for Chris. She hadn't bothered to remove it, thinking no one would notice it on her left hand. How wrong she was. Grace glanced down at her hand. "It's called a Band-Aid."

The woman continued to stare at it as though she just didn't understand. Some doctor. Grace glanced at the image on the Band-Aid. Screw her. "It's Diego. He's an animal rescuer."

Evan let out a choking sound, and she looked up at him. She would die if he looked at her with embarrassment. Instead her breath caught in her throat as those magnificent blue eyes of his were sparkling, and his lips were turned up slightly.

He turned to Alexandra. "Yes, Diego is cousins with Dora."

Alexandra frowned at them. *"Who?"*

This time he broke out into a wide grin. "Dora, the renowned explorer."

Alexandra's pink lips turned into a deep frown before she spoke. "I can see your time in Red River has taken its toll on you, Evan. Well, I'm sure you're counting down the days until you can leave that place. And I'll confess, I am so happy we'll be working together again. You and I, working at Medcorp, will be like old times, except with a hell of a lot more money."

· · ·

Grace hadn't said a word to him in the elevator. The evening had been a complete failure after Alex's manipulations. Well, it had been fine in terms of appearances to everyone at Medcorp, but it had been a disaster for the one person who really mattered.

He slid the key card in the holder and then pushed the door open, waiting for Grace to walk into the suite. She walked past him in a flurry of silk and perfume and then spun around to face him. He forced himself to only let his gaze travel over her for a moment, taking in how lovely she was, even angry. He'd been proud to have her by his side tonight, and she'd mingled beautifully with everyone. Except Alex. "I thought I could keep going, I thought I could handle it. But I can't. I can't keep doing this, Evan."

He swallowed hard. "Doing what?"

Before he could answer, she marched across the room to the washroom. "Whatever it is we're doing. This pretend fiancée thing. This real relationship. Everything. What are we? What's real and what's fake? Is the man I see in Red

River everyday—the one who cares for patients all day, loves his family, treats my son like he's so special, and warms my bed every night—the real, Evan? Or is the man I saw tonight, the one who's about to enter a profession that's all about money, with his ex—whom I must add is a total snot— is that the real you?"

He ran his hand over his jaw and mouth, hating that she was asking him things he didn't know himself. A month ago, he would have known the answer. He wouldn't have been able to imagine being even remotely interested in carrying on with Chalmers's practice. He wouldn't have been able to imagine himself so attached to her son. A month ago, he hadn't known Grace. He hadn't known he could feel this way about anyone. And if he were brutally honest, he wouldn't have known this other side to himself. The side that was soft. The side that gave a damn about so many other things besides his career. He wouldn't have put a relationship above his career. Or a woman.

"You know what else? I think Mrs. Jacobs's wedding was a hell of a lot more fun than tonight. I don't even know why you don't like that poor woman. Calling her crazy. You know who's crazy? Dr. Botox—"

"Who?"

"Alex, that's who—"

Evan choked out a laugh, and an indescribable feeling stole through him as he watched her toss her makeup into her case.

"I also don't like being dressed up like a Barbie doll and having rich old men stare at my cleavage," she continued.

He didn't think it would be a good time to mention that it was impressive cleavage. "Would it help if I told you that

poor old men stare at your cleavage, too?"

She spun on her heel and pointed a can of hair spray in his direction. He backed up a step in case her finger depressed the nozzle. It probably wasn't the best time to tell her about the geriatric pervs back at the clinic.

"And I will not be made to feel inferior because I'm not a doctor or didn't go to school for five thousand years. I'm an artist, and for the record, Dr. Mom is a valid profession. I take my role as a mother very seriously. And you know what else, Evan? I liked you a lot better when you were tossing rocks into the water with Ella and Chris. Sure you look," she paused, looked him up and down and then cleared her throat, "somewhat attractive in a tuxedo—"

He took a step closer to her. "I believe you used the word beautiful before—"

"That was before the gala—"

"Grace, come here," he whispered gruffly.

"No." She slammed the hairspray bottle on the counter and put her hands on her hips. "You come here."

"Gladly," he said and swallowed up the distance between them in one step.

"What are you doing?"

He braced his arms on the marble counter, on either side of her. "You told me to come here. Here I am."

"I was just being argumentative."

"I know, but I took it as the perfect opportunity."

"For what?"

"For this." He leaned over to kiss her. He wanted her. He wanted to hold her in his arms again, wanted to feel her sigh against him, lean on him. He wanted her mouth under his, her bare skin against his. He wanted to not explain the

Medcorp thing. He just wanted to spend the night in this suite making love to her.

"I need answers, everything, Evan. I need to know where this is going." She pulled away from him and walked into the main room. He took a deep breath and followed her out. They needed a glass of something. The champagne tonight didn't seem adequate for the conversation they were about to have. He needed to keep this light and avoid a discussion he didn't have an answer to. He knew this was inevitable. The last few weeks had been more intense than he would have ever imagined. He had never gotten closer to anyone. And he knew by the way she looked at him, by everything she gave him, she felt it, too. And he knew that she would need more. But that's what he hadn't figured out yet.

He walked over to the bar and dropped a few cubes of ice into each crystal tumbler. "Can I get you a drink?"

She shook her head and wrapped her arms around her waist.

"I needed to be here tonight," he said. "I missed it last year because of the accident. I just didn't want to show up here with nothing—"

"I meant us. Where are *we* going?"

This was the question he had no answer to. He squeezed the cool crystal of the glass in one hand and rubbed the nape of his neck with the other. He forced himself to look at Grace, who was standing there, completely open to him. Her green eyes were filled with a distrust that went years beyond him. *Where are we going?*

"We don't have to make decisions tonight."

She turned away, chewing her lip. "We do. I can't keep going, wondering and worrying when it's all going to end—"

"One day at a time—"

She looked down at her shoes. "I can't do it anymore. If I were on my own, maybe. But one day at a time doesn't really work when you have a kid."

His stomach dropped, pushed down by guilt. "Grace—"

"I want details. What are your plans? Your job. Me. Chris."

"I'll be moving back to Toronto as soon as Dr. Chalmers comes back to work."

She broke his stare, but he could see the way she tightened her hold on her stomach. "But what about family practice? There were rumors that Dr. Chalmers was going to retire; there will be a new hospital in Red River in the next few years."

He shrugged. "This is a better move for me career-wise—"

"But what about your family? Staying close to them?"

"I can visit. It's not that far," he said, downing some whiskey. It did nothing to ease the ache in his chest. He was being an ass. She deserved more than the answers he was offering. He had thought—struggled—with the idea of taking over for Chalmers. Doing the whole family man thing with Grace and Chris but then gut-wrenching fear would take over. He would fail her. He had made his decision at a young age what kind of life he wanted, and it wasn't the one she needed.

"I thought…" Her voice trailed, and she walked over to stand in front of the balcony doors. "I thought you might stay in Red River and take over Dr. Chalmers's practice. We worked so well together."

He sighed roughly and walked over to her, standing behind her. "I tried it. It's not for me. I'm sorry if I made you believe otherwise."

"I just thought… You didn't give it a real chance. You tried it, knowing you had this other opportunity. You didn't evaluate it for what it is. A chance to help the people in your hometown, to follow in your mentor's footsteps. Your patients love you. I know the time you put in there. I know you weren't just going through the motions. You care about those people, whether you realize it or not. You didn't have to stay there every night, reviewing tests the day they arrive, setting up referrals with the best specialists. You even pulled strings, calling in favors and changing some of the doctors they were with when you didn't feel things were right. You didn't have to do that. You wouldn't have done any of that if you didn't truly care. I thought being a doctor was your dream. You wouldn't be a doctor if you join Medcorp. You'd be a CEO. How is that anything remotely close to your heart?"

"I take my position at the clinic very seriously. It's what any good doctor would do. I was a kid with silly dreams of being like Dr. Chalmers—"

"So then tell me this is your dream. Tell me that running a clinic accessible only to certain people in a certain income bracket is your dream. That even though you could use your talent as a doctor to help people, you'd rather run this chain of private plastic-surgery clinics. Tell me how you'll help people then? We live in a country that has free healthcare, you have the opportunity to help people in any income bracket, and yet you're choosing the complete opposite. Worse, because you'll just be there shuffling papers! Medcorp isn't even accessible to burn victims or people needing legitimate plastic surgery because of illness. I don't get it. How do you go from freaking out because your temp patients are eating too much sugar, to walking away and being a CEO? It's like you think Red River isn't good enough for you."

Jeezus. He took another drink, and she spun around to look at him.

"Tell me, Evan."

He blinked, the unfamiliar feeling of failure filling him. This is who he was, and he'd never pretended to be otherwise. "At some point, you have to grow up and stop being an idealist. It's great to be a bleeding-heart liberal until you're out there in the real world, and there are bills that need to be paid."

"I don't care how much you make—"

"*I* do. *I* care. I didn't work this hard, sacrifice having a life in order to get ahead, only to wind up in Red River. I need to be the best."

"You are," she whispered, taking a step closer to him. And when he saw the tears fill her eyes, he wanted to believe her, and he wanted to be the man she needed. He wanted to cut off the words he knew were going to hurt her by kissing her and making love to her until neither of could move or remember that this was all supposed to be a temporary arrangement.

"You don't know what you're talking about. You have some naive notion of who I am because of the accident. You put me on the goddamn pedestal that I never asked to be on, and now you're looking at me like I'm a monster."

She shook her head vehemently. "I'm not. I'm not. But what do you expect? You've shared nothing about yourself. The most I learned about you was from Holly and Claire."

He hung his head and set down his drink. For the first time, he felt compelled to get it all out. "Okay, Grace. Fair enough. Here's the truth: When I was kid, I decided I was never going to get married. I was never going to have a family. Or a wife. I was going to leave Red River and be better than my parents and my brother, Jake. Because they were so fucked-up. My father had a tight leash on my mother and made so many bonehead decisions that he ultimately destroyed everything."

"What are you talking about?"

Evan blinked and pushed the words he'd never spoken to anyone through. At the end of all this she was going to hate him anyway. At least he could say he'd been honest. He rolled his shoulders, trying to shrug off the sudden wave of unease as it crashed over him. Honesty, feelings, and the whole thing were highly overrated if this is what they did to a person.

Grace was looking at him with her head tilted, a tiny amount of hope lighting her green eyes. He'd be the one quashing that light out in a few seconds. "Last year, I found out that everything about my family had been a lie. Jake told us that he wasn't our father's son. When he was a kid, he overheard my parents arguing. My mother had been raped. And, uh," his throat constricted and he stared up at the ceiling, blinking away the emotion, "they had contemplated aborting him. And my father hated him from the day he was born, and our mother, just…tried her best."

"Oh, Evan," Grace whispered. She wrapped her arms around him, all softness and sweetness. And just like every damn time he held this woman in his arms, he prayed that he could be what she needed. That she could somehow chip away at the man he'd become, and that someone else would appear, someone that was worthy of her. Grace gave herself to whoever needed her. She put everyone's needs above hers and saw the good. She was soft and so goddamn sweet that he knew they wouldn't be able to last. He wanted to stand by her and love her and soak it all in, every sweet morsel she offered him, but it wouldn't be fair. He placed his hands on her shoulders, gently pushing her away.

He took a deep breath; he was going to finish and then end this. "I didn't know any of that growing up. All I knew was that Jake caused my parents a hell of a lot of pain. He was always in trouble with the police, and our mother would… just stand there at the window, waiting, pacing, crying and wait for him to come home. I could never understand. My father drilled into me that Jake was a complete disappointment, and it was my job to not turn out like him. To push myself and do better, be the best. '*Don't settle for anything but the best, Evan. Get out of this town, make something of yourself.*' Our mother was tortured. She wanted to love Jake. But my father…he hated him."

He reached for his glass and downed the last of the whiskey. *Finish this, Evan.* "And for a long time, I think I hated him, too. Then when I found out the truth, I hated myself even more. I had spent so many years resenting Jake, thinking he was the cause of all of our problems growing up. But the truth was, he'd been carrying this goddamn lie his entire life. And Jake is a good man. Better than I could ever be."

"Evan, you didn't know, you can't blame yourself. And I know you. You're a good man—"

"It doesn't matter now. I've gone down this road, this path I laid out for myself a long time ago. And it doesn't involve marriage, or kids. And I'm sorry if you thought this was permanent or—"

Grace's gasp, her physical step back from him robbed him of any more words. He squeezed his eyes shut because it hurt like hell to look at her. He was the biggest kind of asshole. But in the end, he was doing her a favor. He needed to remember that.

· · ·

Grace's chest heaved with each small breath she took. It hurt to look at him, to speak to him, to be so close to Evan and not know him. "You're not the man who saved us from the car. That man risked his life to save a woman and little boy he didn't even know. After they pulled me out of the car, you stayed. You stayed when his seat belt was *caught*."

His handsome features were drawn, the mouth that had passionately, tenderly made love to her all night was pulled into a grim line. She was frantically trying to process everything he was saying and trying to keep whatever they had from self-imploding.

"Your father pulled a number on you," she whispered, tears making it difficult to speak.

He paused, refilling his glass. "What are you talking about?"

"He brainwashed you. Because of his own inadequacies, he off-loaded that onto you. He drilled in the need for you to excel, to be the best, to skip grades and do more, faster, and forfeit your childhood."

"You're wrong. I wanted to be a doctor. *Me.* That wasn't his idea. I'm the one who followed Chalmers around every day after school. I wanted to be just like him."

"Then why aren't you? Why is the thought of taking over his practice seen as a failure to you?"

"I don't know; it's just not good enough anymore."

She nodded, trying not to panic. "Okay. So you don't

want to stay in Red River. You don't want the practice. What
do you want, then?" She didn't dare breathe, not really be-
lieving she'd had the courage to ask that question. *Please say
me. Please say you want me and Chris.* She watched, motionless as he swore under his breath and broke her stare. Acid
churned in her stomach until she burned with the agony of
Evan's rejection.

She swallowed hard and wiped the tears from her eyes.
"That shelter, across the street from the new Medcorp office
is the one my mother and I always went to."

"Grace—"

"No. I've been broke, and I've been homeless. And my
mother taught me that all you have left in life when you've
lost everything else are your principles, your beliefs. You can
have money, Evan, but if you've lost the man inside, you've
got nothing." She waited for her words to sink in. She prayed
for them to sink in. But those blue eyes weren't soft. They
were cool and distant.

"That's a beautiful theory. But it doesn't have to be so
black and white. Everyone can choose a different path. Not
everyone is cut out to be a saint-in-training."

"What?" She knew she was shaking, her muscles
trembling like a rock climber's almost at the top of her
ascent. She was humiliating herself. The man couldn't make
it any clearer that she had been nothing but a fling for him.
*Stupid, stupid fool, Grace.*

He looked down into his glass for a moment and then
up at her. "I can't offer you what you want. But we can still
see each other."

Hurt and shame slashed through her body, making
it almost impossible to stand up. To look at him. But she

needed to know—before she walked out of here—if he loved her at all. She lifted her chin and squared her shoulders even though they felt as though they were being held down by invisible weights. "That's not good enough."

Evan's tanned skin dropped a few shades lighter. "I'm not good enough?"

She shook her head. "Your offer. It's not good enough for me anymore. Or Christopher. Maybe it's insane; maybe it's completely unrealistic, and it will never happen, but we need to be number one in someone's life. Chris has been number one to me since the day I knew I was pregnant. But to no one else. And I have never been number one to anyone. But Chris and I deserve that."

"Grace, I will always help you if you need something—"

"Money isn't enough. I can provide that now. I have a job, and I have my art career finally starting. I don't need a lot. I don't need the kind of money you're offering. I want your heart, Evan. I want you to tell me that you love me, my son, and that we can be together forever." Her voice cracked on that last bit, but she wouldn't stop. She was going for home. She'd never been this close to true love, to perfection, and she was going to give it her all, even if it killed her.

His face had taken on a gray color, every line completely drawn as he stood there, straight and tall, powerful and smart as hell. But so empty.

"Grace—"

She held up her hand and let the tears that were clogging her throat fall. "I love you. My little boy loves you. And I need that. I will support you, we would follow you, support your dreams whatever they were, but I need your love."

That strong jaw just clenched incessantly, and she

searched his eyes, looking for the tiniest hint of the emotion that filled her body, consumed her. She had just told him she loved him, and he didn't say a word. "Maybe it's hard to love another man's child. I don't know. I will forever be thankful to you, always grateful to you for rescuing us. But I messed up once for Chris. I can't do it again."

He was shaking his head. "I don't need your gratitude—"

She wrung her hands together and the only voice that was left inside her came out as a whisper. "You promised me that you wouldn't let Chris get attached to you."

"I'm not the one walking away here, Grace."

"Really? That's what you think? You're not even *here*. I'm here. I'm telling you that I love you, and you can't even say the words back. So you know what? Yeah, I'm leaving. I've known three men in my life. I haven't been good enough for any of you to stick around. I'm done with that. This time, *I* walk out."

Ugly silence filled the gorgeous room; the only sound was Grace moving, collecting her things. She stood at the doorway for a moment.

"Grace, let me drive you home." Her hand shook on the doorknob. She'd wanted him to say he was wrong, that he loved her. She didn't care how the hell she got home.

"Screw you for treating us so well. You were everything I ever dreamed about in a man, in a father for Christopher. Screw you for making love to me like I was the only woman you'd ever wanted. This…what you did—" Her voice broke, and she ignored his tortured voice when he said her name. *Get out, Grace, before you cave.* "The last thing I want is your courtesy. I'll find my own way home, Evan."

# Chapter Fourteen

Evan stood on the street corner of one of downtown Toronto's most posh neighborhoods. The walk signal on the street corner lit, and the pedestrians around him moved like faceless drones, brushing against his shoulder as he stood still. He blinked. And suddenly, the designer shops disappeared, the imported cars faded away, and immaculately dressed people blurred to nothing.

He frowned, opening his umbrella as chilly spring rain splattered down from the sky and onto the street and sidewalks. He needed to move. He needed to get to his meeting. This morning, he would officially be made CEO of Medcorp, and all his ties to Grace would essentially be severed.

Lambert had called him the day after the gala, and just like that, everything Evan had ever wanted was handed to him. Except he was hungover, sitting on the marble floor in the hotel bathroom, and the glory of victory didn't hit him. Not then, and not a few minutes later when he hurled into the toilet.

He forced himself to put one foot in front of the other, pounding the pavement. If he could physically get to the building, then he could pull off the rest. *Just focus, Evan.* Never mind the distractions, the new sights he was witnessing. But even as he thought it, his eyes didn't stay focused on the reality in front of him. Instead he saw Grace. And Christopher. Grace, kissing Evan's scars, healing his soul. And Christopher holding his hand, telling him that if he ever had a dad, he wished it would be just like Evan. The accident, the memory of Grace and Christopher in that car, consumed him until he choked on it.

Evan shoved his hands in his pockets and discovered the item he'd apparently been carrying around since Grace had walked out on him. He pulled it out of his interior suit pocket and held it in his hands. The Spider-Man notepad. He flipped through it that night, his gut churning as he read all the items—in chronological order from the first day she'd arrived in Red River. The words tortured him. *Meet Dr. Evan Manning…Thank Dr. Evan Manning…Give Dr. Manning muffins…Go shopping with Evan…Go to first day of work (don't screw it up)…Go to wedding…Thank Evan…*thank him for what?

Anger and regret filled him until he was sure he would explode. Grace always had a fight in her. She was always proud and in control. But seeing the tears and the dejection on her face that night tore at him and had haunted him since last week. He'd done the right thing in leaving, but he'd hurt her.

Rain tumbled onto the street, pedestrians walking faster, jumping over puddles. But all he could focus on was the image of Grace crying in front of him, holding up her hand as though she needed to stop an attacker tormented him. He had never been a man to make a woman cry. He'd never let a woman close enough to him to cause that kind of pain.

The last woman he'd seen so destroyed had been his mother, whenever she'd be waiting by the window for his brother Jake to come home. Evan could still remember the exact sound of her sobs, the look of anguish on her face when his older brother would stumble through the door, wasted and angry. His father's words echoed in his mind: *Don't be a screw-up like your brother, Jake. You understand, Evan? You're better than that. Don't disappoint us.* Evan squeezed his eyes shut. He'd spent his entire life excelling at everything. He'd skipped two grades, finished his undergrad early. He'd been conditioned to excel. But doing so now meant he'd failed the most important person in his life.

She'd get over him. It was better this way.

The sea of black trench coats and briefcases, nameless, faceless people passed by. The jarring brush of a shoulder against him, as he stood still in the parade, shook him from his thoughts, forcing him to action.

He took a deep breath and looked up at the Medcorp building, squinting as the sun bounced off the wall of glass. This was what he'd wanted. This was the path he'd chosen. He rode the elevator, staring blankly at the numbers as it coasted to the fiftieth floor. And then he walked into the pristine, stunningly modern offices of Medcorp. A jaw-dropping view of the city was the backdrop to the waiting room. Sleek leather chairs, glass-and-steel tables, and perfectly poised, coiffed patients. No creaking floors, just polished marble. No zany, raincoat wearing, pastry-eating patients, just society's elite. He walked toward the massive, curved steel reception desk and forced a smile on his face as a tall, blonde woman rose and gave him the most composed smile. There wasn't a hint of genuine emotion as she greeted him. Her hair was pulled into a sleek knot without even the tiniest strand askew.

"Dr. Manning, how wonderful to meet you. Welcome."

He didn't maintain eye contact, because he was busy noting the immaculate surface of her desk. There wasn't a picture of a mischievous four-year-old or potato-chip crumbs or a Spider-Man notepad. This desk was pure perfection. And a month ago he would have been impressed.

Minutes later he was entering his office. The door swung open, not sticking and creaking. It was a sprawling, lavish corner office. Floor-to-ceiling windows. Glass. Steel. He chucked his briefcase onto a leather chair and jammed his hands into his pockets, walking over to the windows. A million-dollar view. Problem was, in the last month he'd found an entirely different million-dollar view: in the form of a gorgeous, curvy, green-eyed goddess who had bravely told him his offer wasn't good enough for her anymore, who had taught him more about what was important in his life than anyone.

"We've come a long way, haven't we, Evan?"

Evan's muscles stiffened at the sound of Alexandra's cultured voice. His day was going from bad to worse. The only way he had a chance in hell at salvaging it would be to walk the hell out of here. A waft of Alexandra's overly sweet perfume filled the room, and the sound of her heels clicking against the tiles indicated she hadn't noted—or cared—about his lack of greeting. Somehow she managed to fit herself in the small amount of space between himself and the window. She reached out and settled her hands on his lapels as she smiled at him, and he knew: Alex was his past. She was a woman who symbolized everything he once was.

And God, did it hurt to look at her.

Almost as much as it hurt to look at himself in the mirror after letting Grace go.

It hit him then that he'd been all wrong about moving forward. For him, it meant going back to the place he started from.

He grasped Alex's cool hands in his and removed them from his body, taking a step back. A step in the right direction. For once, he was going in the right direction. "I'm done. I'm walking out of here, and I'm going home."

"But, Evan," she said, a tiny crease appearing above her eyes where normal people her age had worry lines. "This is what you've always wanted."

"I know. And aren't I an idiot for only figuring out now that I was all wrong? I don't want any of this."

He turned around and walked out on everything he ever thought he wanted.

It was time to go home. To Grace and Christopher. To his family. To Red River.

• • •

Two hours later, Evan burst through Dr. Chalmers's clinic doors like some fop in a black-and-white movie about to save the town. He didn't even care. His eyes were focused on the empty desk and disappointment anchored him in the doorway. It took a moment before for the commotion in the room registered. One side of the waiting room was filled with Mrs. Jacobs, Mr. Puccini, their significant others… and Sheila. She was back from her cruise and judging by the lobster-esque glow of her skin, had failed to use sunscreen. He frowned because no one had even noticed him—they were all bending over tying up their shoelaces. He did a double take at a familiar-looking young man. Chicken boy. He was here. With flowers…seated beside Mr. McCann who was also holding a bouquet of flowers. Seriously? He'd been gone a week, and these two were moving in on Grace?

He scowled at them. Chicken boy squirmed in his seat, and his face grew red.

McCann just glowered at him. "You snooze, you lose, Doctor."

Evan turned his back to them and assessed the rest of the situation.

The other side was filled with his family, and he avoided looking at them. The entire place was packed with people who had known him his entire life, and he'd never felt so alone. He wanted some of his brothers' snarky comments and useless advice. How many times when he'd been alone in the city or coming back after a double shift at the hospital had he just wanted a beer with one or both of them? He'd fooled himself for so long into thinking what he needed was to be the best. And that his family was just an addition to the life he was leading. Sure he'd always loved them, and he'd visited often. He'd been around for the birth of their children. But he'd distanced himself from Quinn and Jake. They ran their business together, saw each other day in and day out, and he was always on the sidelines. He rolled his shoulders and took a deep breath. He was going to turn everything around. He was going to be the guy Grace believed he was. He was home, and it felt right.

He cleared his throat, and everyone looked up, and suddenly it was the typical mayhem. Even old Eunice didn't irritate him. Even when she stood and hiked up her dress, showing him way more leg than needed. It took him a minute to register that she was pointing at her foot. A bright pink Nike sneaker with orange laces nearly blinded him. "We're going on our daily walk!"

Mr. Puccini rose, chest puffed. "Because of you, Dr. Evan, we started a walking club. That sweet Grace thought it was a perfect idea—we ran it by her, of course. We meet here at four every afternoon, doing a big lap around the downtown, over the river front—"

"And then reward ourselves with cannoli at Natalia's!"

He shouldn't have grinned, condoning this flawed logic, but he did.

"Evan, I didn't expect to see you here. Didn't think they'd let you leave work so early in the day?" Evan met Dr. Chalmers's cautious gaze from the doorway.

He ran his hands through his hair. "I, uh, resigned." He ignored the gasps and kept speaking. "I probably should have lined up something else before doing that, but, uh, I was thinking there might be a place for me here."

And just like that Chalmers's weathered face cracked into a broad grin. "This is your home, dear boy. I'm happy you finally figured it out. I was worried about how much longer I'd have to keep working. But I had knew you'd be back," he said with a wink. He lifted up his leg and showed off bright white sneakers. "Time for me to take care of myself and enjoy retirement."

He walked across the room and gave Evan a hearty slap on the back.

Evan glanced at the slightly disorganized reception desk. Everything exactly where it should be. Potted, slightly dying plant perched on the edge. A picture of Chris grinning like he'd just pulled off a major coup staring back at him. Everything was as it should be, almost. Evan cleared his throat. "Where's Grace?"

"She's probably typing up her resignation notice!"

He counted to ten and turned to Sheila. "If that were the case, then she'd be sitting at her desk. Typing."

Sheila leaned over to Eunice and attempted a whisper. "See what I mean about the patronizing?"

Evan turned to his family, hoping for some help. "She's gone, Ev." Fear slammed through him, and it took him several long moments for it to register that Jake was smiling.

Claire shoved Jake and gave him a compassionate smile. "Grace is in the back room getting her things. We're on our way to a picnic."

Evan breathed a sigh of relief. He had always felt like an outsider among his family, but never more than today. He'd spent his entire life excelling at everything. He'd skipped grades, finished his undergrad early. He'd been conditioned to excel. And yet he'd failed, in the most important aspect of his life. He had been the only one of his brothers incapable of love, until Grace. He stood there in his suit and tie and silently cursed himself for ever thinking he needed anything more than the people sitting here.

Chris barreled through the hallway and into the waiting room, took one look at him, and dove into his arms. Without hesitating, Evan scooped him up. His heart constricted painfully as Chris's arms wrapped around his neck, just as they had the day of the accident, small and trusting. This kid…had worked his way into his heart, and had made him a better man. Christopher had seen something in him, right from day one. Chris had believed in him, when he himself didn't even know what or who he was. And now it was his turn. He needed to be there for Christopher and Grace…if she took him back.

"I'm so glad you came back, Nevan. I knew you would."

Evan squeezed his eyes shut for a moment and pushed out words from his mouth that felt so right. "I never want to leave you again, Chris."

Christopher jumped down and gave him a smile with wattage only he was capable of. Evan ignored the sound of loud nose blowing behind him and made his third attempt at walking down the hall to find Grace. "I knew it. Even when I saw you sneaking out of our house every morning at four o'clock, I knew you'd come back. Maybe now, if you explain to my mom that you're here for good, you won't have to sneak anymore."

Evan's mouth dropped open, and he ignored the snorts and snickers coming from behind him—his brothers no doubt. The gasps were courtesy of Eunice and her crew. Evan opened his mouth to answer when Grace appeared in the doorway. Her hair was up in a ponytail, slightly crazy, completely sexy. He physically ached for her, being so close to her, knowing that he'd failed her.

Grace's green eyes were on him, and though he'd expected to see anger in them, it wasn't there. No, it was the unmistakable sheen of disappointment and hurt.

"Grace." His voice sounded hoarse to his own ears. She

still didn't say anything. And then she lifted her chin and walked right on by him, to her desk.

"Good afternoon, Doctor Manning. I'm sorry but there aren't any appointments left today."

Again, snickers and snorts from the Peanut Gallery behind him, followed this time by an overzealous "You go, girl" from Eunice. He stood in front of the desk, aware that Holly and Claire were trying to occupy the kids and give them privacy.

Grace was shuffling papers on her desk, a Diego notepad peeking out from under a bouquet of roses. The card stapled to the cellophane wrapping said Congratulations.

"Celebrating?"

Grace didn't say anything.

So his brother, Quinn, decided to answer what he'd thought was a quiet, private question. "Someone bought Grace's entire collection of black-and-white sketches, even before her show."

Evan turned around to look at him. Quinn settled a hard gaze on him. Funny how Quinn could still evoke older-brother *I'm-going-to-beat-the-crap-out-of-you* intimidation on him.

Jake snorted. "What a moron. The gallery was going to do a promotion for 15 percent off that night since she's a new artist."

Evan studied both his brothers, wondering if they knew. Two seconds later, it was confirmed. Quinn looked away, and Jake couldn't keep his grin off his face.

"You know, Evan, if you didn't act like such an ass, maybe Grace would have given them to you for a better discount."

Evan would have laughed, if the situation weren't so damn pitiful. Or if Grace hadn't snapped her head up to look at him. *She* hadn't known it was him. Though it wasn't her fault, that hurt. She hadn't realized those sketches meant anything to him. She had no idea just how much she and Christopher meant.

"I'll buy them!" Chicken boy yelled out, standing at attention.

"They're sold. Keep up with the conversation," Evan snapped, scaring the boy into sitting down again.

He walked over to where she was standing, behind the desk, the weight of the silence and his family's stares slowing him.

"I'm sorry, Grace."

She sighed and looked somewhere beyond his shoulder.

He jammed his hands into his pockets. "I walked out of Medcorp today."

Her eyes connected with his, her full lips parting gently. "Pardon?"

He clenched his jaw and nodded. "Didn't look back. I'm here for good. I'll be taking over the clinic. I'm staying in Red River, and I swear to God, I'll do whatever it takes to earn your trust again."

"Well, then give'r a ring, hotshot!"

McCann. Evan narrowed his eyes on him. "I'm upping your physio to five days a week."

He caught the slight softening in Grace's eyes as she studied him. He took a step closer to her, so that he could feel her, smell her. His hands ran the length of her bare arms until he cupped her face. "If you let me, I want to help you fulfill your dreams, Grace. You are so gifted, and I want you to taste what's it's like to have your dreams come true. Because that's what you've done for me."

She squeezed her eyes shut, and he hoped his words were enough.

"You know that night that Christopher was sick?" he whispered, looking down into her glittering green eyes as she opened them. "Chris told me that an angel rescued you two."

She looked down.

"I think it's the other way around," he said gruffly, emotion constricting his throat. He leaned down, his lips hovering over hers. "You and Chris saved me, Grace. I know enough about myself to know that. But I am not the same man who would put everything else above family. I lived and breathed my career. Being at the top of my profession—it was everything for me. But I know that all those things, titles, mean nothing when you are standing in front of me, right now. I want you, Christopher, and any other children if we decide we want them. I want to live with you forever. I want to buy the house on the river from my brothers, and I want you to have the coach house for your studio. I want to love you and make love to you every day and make up for every shitty day you ever had. I love you."

She leaned forward, and he clasped the back of her head to his chest, feeling the moisture seeping through his shirt. He kissed the top of her head, and then slowly she pulled away to look at him. "I begged you, Evan. I stood there, after laying it all out, telling you that I loved you and you let me walk away."

He winced. And then kneeled on the ground. At least behind the damn desk they could get some privacy.

"What are you doing?" she whispered.

"I'm not above begging you or apologizing for failing you. I want to be your rock, and if you let me, I will never fail you again. I want you to hold my hand and know that you and Christopher can count on me. I want to be the man in your sketchbook."

He held his breath as she covered her face.

The moment was ruined by Eunice. "My dear, have some self-respect—"

"Ah, man, Ev! Again with the kneeling? What is it with you two? There are kids in the room." Evan didn't even bother turning around to yell at Jake. He just stared up at Grace and raised his other hand from behind the desk and flipped his brother the finger.

"I love you, too," she said, sinking onto the ground and into his arms.

He captured her mouth, the sound of her declaration, the sweetness in her voice filling all the little hollows inside with love.

Cheers and hooting, along with an, "Atta boy, Evan," courtesy of his brothers, filled the room.

"I thought I knew pain, and I'd hoped I lived my darkest days, but when I left you. God, Evan, I'd never felt to empty or so alone," she whispered against his mouth.

"I'm so sorry. I was an idiot for letting you go. I want to marry you, Grace. A real wedding. Big, small, whatever you want. But I want to stand up in front of our family, friends, and our son and say that I love you. That I want to spend the rest of my life with you and Chris. Because you are the love of my life, Grace."

"Hold out for a ring, dearie! You know what they say about getting the milk without buying the—"

"Can you people give us some privacy?"

Grace was wiping her eyes, and Evan had no idea if

she was crying tears of happiness or pain brought on by his family and townspeople.

"I think you've just earned a spot on my To-Do list again, Evan. I should probably also tell you that when you piss me off at work, I steal a couple of the chips from the sandwich plate you get delivered for lunch."

"Good girl!" Sheila hollered. "I'm glad you took my advice in the notes I left! You should hold out for better work hours and a longer lunch break."

Evan laughed, pulling Grace against him as he kissed her. He ignored Jake yelling out some smart-ass comment, the nose blowing, the muffled comments, and everything else just faded as Grace wrapped her arms around him. His lips locked onto hers and she tasted of their past, their future, their promise.

"Omigod! Holly's water just broke!"

· · ·

They were all hovering around Holly, who was sitting with a blanket wrapped around her. Eunice was giving her breathing and labor advice, even though everyone damn well knew she'd never had a baby.

Quinn yanked him over to the side. "Evan, listen to me. Nothing can happen to Holly or the baby."

"Well, then I suggest you pry Eunice off her."

"I'm serious—"

"So am I. Clear this room."

Minutes later he, Quinn, and Jake had emptied the room of everyone that wasn't family. "Now, relax," he said to his brother, locking the door after Eunice left. "Nothing's going to happen—" he whispered, wishing his brother would keep his voice down before he freaked his wife out. "I've called 9-1-1; there's going to be a police escort meeting us en route—"

"No, you don't get it. I can't live if something happens to either of them. She's my life, man, and if something happens—"

"Nothing is going to happen," Evan said again, placing his hand on his brother's shoulder, looking him squarely in the eye. "But you've got to haul ass and stop acting like a pansy, or she'll freak out. It'll take at least half an hour to get to the regional hospital in Millington."

"Let's go already," Holly yelled.

Evan shoved his normally calm-and-collected brother over to his wife. "You guys go to the car. Grace and I will follow right behind. Jake, you and Claire get all the stuff and meet us at the hospital."

"Mommy's having a baby!" Ella yelled racing in and out of them. Grace yanked Christopher over to her, just as he was about to follow Ella.

"Ella, why don't you ride with us?" Claire called out.

They walked to the cars, every few minutes or so slowing when Holly had a contraction. "Evan, get over here," Quinn yelled. Evan cursed quietly. It was always the most level-headed guys who flaked out when their wives were in labor. Every. Freaking. Time.

"Will she make it to the hospital in time?"

Evan nodded. "I'm pretty sure. But we'll be behind you the whole way. Worst-case scenario, I'll deliver your kid on the side of the road."

Quinn grabbed him by the shoulders. "Are you kidding

me?"

"No, but I'm sure it won't come to that. For the record, man, you were texting me all week about her contractions. Today? What? Nothing?"

His brother's mouth turned into a grim line.

Evan slapped him on the shoulder. "Everything will be fine if you stop talking and drive your wife to the damn hospital."

Finally, it seemed, Quinn got his balls back and ran to the car.

Grace turned to him. "Evan, can I have your car keys?"

He paused. "You're going to drive?"

Grace nodded. "It's time to start over," she whispered. "Next week, I want to drive myself to that gallery. I want to walk in there, and I want to do it by myself. You go with Holly and Quinn—I don't think he should be driving," she said with a laugh.

"Yeah…I love you, Grace."

"I know. I'd feel a little better if your car weren't a BMW, but I think we'll be okay," she said, standing on her tiptoes to give him a kiss. Minutes later they were on their way to the hospital.

• • •

An hour later, after Holly was settled into a delivery room, Grace and Evan took Chris to the park outside the hospital. She couldn't wait for her son to hear the news. She held Evan's hand and felt the light tremor, the reminder of everything he'd sacrificed for them.

"Chris, why don't we sit on this bench?"

Christopher nodded and sat in between them. "This is so cool that Ella's mom is having a baby, don't you think?"

"Yup. Means I'm going to be an uncle again," Evan said.

Christopher looked up at him. "That's cool."

"Yeah, I think being a dad would be even cooler. And being a husband, too."

Christopher frowned at both of them. "Well, then you should."

"I'd like to be your dad. And I'd like to marry your mom."

Grace's throat clogged and she didn't know how she was going to be able to speak.

"My dad?" Christopher whispered, staring at Evan.

Evan nodded, smiling, slightly. The tension in his body was obvious, as he waited for Christopher to say something.

"I always wanted a dad. Ever since I was a little kid," Christopher whispered, staring at Evan with large eyes. "And I never wanted to tell Mom that, in case she got sad. Because she couldn't be a dad. She was a mom, and she couldn't get me a dad. But she was good enough." Evan swallowed repeatedly, and his jaw clenched tight. It was when she saw the tears in his eyes as he stared at their son that she was unable to hold onto hers.

Evan cleared his throat twice before he spoke. "I'm sorry I couldn't be around sooner for you. But I am now. And I'll be your dad forever and ever, okay?"

"And I can be your kid forever, right?"

Evan cleared his throat and nodded. "Forever. And you know what? I always wanted a little boy. And you're the best little boy I could have ever asked for. And I'm so happy and so proud to have you as my son, Christopher."

Christopher threw himself into Evan's arms, and he picked him up, standing. Grace sat on a bench and watched them as tears poured from her eyes. Her son was a remarkable little boy, and it was in his responses to Evan that she knew how badly he'd secretly wanted a father. But he'd always made her feel good enough. And Evan. He was the man she always knew existed. Christopher and Evan held onto each other tightly, and Christopher pulled back to look at Evan. Grace was mesmerized by the sight of them together. Her men.

"You're crying?" Christopher asked. Evan gave him a nod and swiped at the tears that he'd shed. "I didn't think dads cried."

"Well, I don't usually. But I'm really happy today. I'm the happiest I have ever been, because I have you and your mom," he said gruffly.

"Oh, me too. Sometimes I cry," Christopher said.

"Yeah?" Evan said, smoothing his hand over Christopher's head.

Christopher nodded. "I try not to because I'm a big kid now, but sometimes if I get in trouble I cry. Like last month, I found all these toads at the pond by the park and put them in my pocket with dirt and grass, and I thought it would be really cool to have them sleep in my room with me. But I just knew Mom was going to say no, so I sneaked them. So when mom was emptying my pants to do laundry, all this dirt came out, and she asked me what I'd been doing. I was scared I was going to get in trouble, so I lied and said I didn't know. But then mom almost stepped on a toad and then she got all scared and screamed, and I got into huge trouble. We had to search for all the toads and then I had to bring them all back outside."

"Wow. That sounds pretty crazy." Grace could tell Evan was trying to keep a straight face as Christopher talked his head off. "I did something like that once," Evan said, sitting at the table. "Except my older brother, Quinn, found all the snakes before my parents did and helped me bring them back out into the field."

"Cool. I wish I had a brother," Christopher said.

Grace tried not to gasp. She made eye contact with Evan, and he smiled at her, but didn't say a word.

"Well, you have uncles. And aunts. And you have two cousins."

"Cousins?"

"You know Ella and Michael?"

Christopher nodded rapidly. "They're my cousins?"

Evan smiled. "Yup. And their parents are your aunts and uncles. Their dads are my brothers."

"This is so cool. The coolest day I ever had in my whole life. Are we all going to live together like a family? And do all the things that real families do? Like are you going to read me stories at night? And then we're all going to have dinner together? And you can show me how to pick up snakes and stuff? Mom hates snakes! And she doesn't like spiders either." Christopher looked over at her, and she smiled at him. Then he whispered loudly in Evan's ear. "She pretends she's not afraid of them, but I know she is."

Evan laughed and squeezed Christopher to his chest. "We'll do all of those things. And lots more. You've got to tell me all about your favorite things, okay?"

"You're going to be a really cool dad. Wait till I tell my friend, Will, at school, that I have a dad now, too. His dad takes him fishing. Do you like fishing? I started taking swimming lessons, and my mom said when I know how to swim we could go on a boat and fish. But I don't really think she likes fish. I mean, she's scared of spiders, so I don't see how she's going to like slimy fish, you know?"

Evan's face was filled with pride and wonder as he listened to *their* son.

For the first time since her mother had been alive, everything felt perfect. Everything as it should be. For the first time in her life, she felt that anything was possible. She was going to pursue her painting. Her dreams. She was going to conquer the last of her demons. And their son would know, through their mistakes, that love was enough, more than enough to inspire even the most difficult dreams.

• • •

After a long day in the waiting room with Claire, Jake, Evan, and the kids, a haggard but beaming Quinn had come out with the news that Holly had safely delivered a healthy baby girl. They all cried and hugged, and Grace shared in their joy.

"It's a good thing Holly had that baby so quickly, or I think Quinn would've been the next patient," Evan said, as they walked toward the maternity wing of the hospital.

"So this baby is my cousin, too, right?" Christopher was walking beside them, insistent that he be the one to carry the pink dinosaur while Evan carried the pink roses.

"That's right. Baby Jennifer Manning is the newest addition to the family, Chris."

"What a pretty name," Grace said.

"It's in honor of Holly's sister, Jennifer."

"How special. I'm so happy for them," Grace whispered as they reached Holly's room.

"Me, too, sweetheart," Evan whispered, kissing her temple.

Evan grabbed the back of Chris's shirt, laughing as he was about to burst through the door. "Knock first, Chris."

Christopher nodded, knocked, and seconds later, Quinn swung open the door with a huge grin on his handsome face.

Grace looked around the hospital room, holding onto her breath, because the emotion that coursed through her was so powerful when she saw Holly in bed, holding her baby girl. Claire was in a chair beside her, and Jake was standing next to her. Grace was amazed by how perfectly comfortable she was with everyone.

"You know that this means?" Ella asked, jumping up and down as she spotted Chris. Michael toddled over to stand next to Chris.

Christopher crossed his arms. "What?"

"Now it's two girls against two boys! We're even," she said with a mischievous smile.

Everyone laughed, and Grace focused her eyes on the family that filled the room. The people that had accepted her unconditionally and without judgment. These were people that wouldn't leave, that wouldn't walk out when the going got rough. Once you were their family, they were there for the long haul, and you wouldn't be able to get rid of them if you tried. They'd have her back, and she'd have theirs. She had never known family like this, until Evan. She leaned back against him, his arms instantly wrapping around her, like she knew would happen. But it was a feeling she would never tire of.

"Maybe my mom and dad can have a kid," Christopher whispered loudly to Ella.

"I didn't know you have a dad!"

Christopher nodded, his chest swelling. "Yeah. Nevan's my dad."

Ella's eyes grew wide. "Uncle Evan is your *dad?* Why am I always the last to know?"

"It's okay. I just found out, too. So we're going to be living here now. I heard them talking and Neva—Dad said that he's going to ask your dad if he can buy that house beside the one we're living at. And he said, that he was going to ask for a family discount."

Everyone burst out laughing.

• • •

While Grace walked over to chat with Claire and Holly, Evan went to stand next to Jake.

"I, uh, I just wanted to say I'm sorry."

Jake turned his head sharply to him. "For what?"

He needed to do this in a way that wouldn't reveal anything that would hurt Jake, but enough that he could finally feel like he could clear his conscience. "For doubting the kind of man you were. For not being there for you."

This time, he did hold his brother's gaze, and he looked into the eyes that were so similar to his. Similar, yet different because of what their eyes had seen. He saw it for a second—the flash of the kid he once was. "You don't owe me an apology, Ev."

"I do. I just want you to know that for what it's worth, you and Quinn are right up there. The best guys I know." Jake didn't say anything for a moment, but a sheen of moisture appeared and then was blinked away quickly.

Jake punched his arm. "Of course we are. Right alongside you."

He could have reached out to hug his brother, but the way Jake was standing, it didn't really look like it would be welcome. And that was fine. Easier that way.

Instead they both looked over at Quinn who was wiping his eyes.

Jake nudged his chin in Quinn's direction. "Freaking fiftieth time I've seen him cry today."

"Pfft. Tell me about it. We should buy him a box of tissues for his next birthday. A pink box."

Jake snorted. "Good idea."

Evan cleared his throat, eyes on Quinn's dopey expression. "Something about babies I guess."

Jake sighed this time and looked at Michael. "I think I cried when Michael was born."

Evan cleared his throat, watching Quinn kiss his new baby girl. "Yeah. I guess I might have cried when Christopher called me Dad."

"I'm glad you're staying in Red River. And I, uh, think you'll make a good father and husband. Maybe a little anal, but…"

He laughed. Things were back to normal. A new normal anyway.

Evan walked over to Grace and wrapped his arms around her. She smiled, and he kissed her, thinking he'd never get tired of this. He'd never get tired of them, and he didn't know what kind of fool he was before to think that nothing could come as close to his career.

He looked down at his new niece as he held the woman who'd changed his life in his arms.

"Holly," he said, his voice loud enough that everyone ceased their chatter and looked at him. He stared into his sister-in-law's exhausted but sparkling eyes and remembered the night he'd gone to help her when Ella had been sick. How long ago that had seemed. How afraid and how different Holly had been. But the woman he was looking at today was strong and courageous. And he knew the daughter she was holding in her arms would one day be the same. Holly was smiling at him, waiting.

"You once—*actually no*—you told me many times that everything happens for a reason. And I disputed your theory over and over again. Well, I'm officially telling you that you were right."

He tightened his hold around Grace and extended his hand, until he felt his son's small hand grasp his. In his touch, he felt the trust and the love and he knew that he and Christopher were connected in a way that could never be taken away. And as he looked down at Grace, at the unconditional love that made her eyes sparkle and her smile even more beautiful, he knew that she'd saved him.

# Epilogue

Grace blinked back tears as she and Christopher stood at the top of the altar. She signaled for him to remain here for a moment. She wanted to savor this, before it was all over. She wanted to embrace where she had come from, where Christopher had come from, and their journey to this place today. To the man that was waiting for them at the altar. Evan's blue eyes held hers, down the rose-petal-filled aisle, his gaze locked onto her and wouldn't let go. Like the first day they'd met.

There wasn't a day that went by that she didn't remember that accident. The burning smell of exhaust and oil still haunted her dreams at night, and the sound of that man's cry still had the power to stop her heart. Sometimes she relived that day as a reminder of all the things she had to be grateful for. And sometimes she relived that day as a reminder of what she'd come so close to losing. Something so beautiful sprang from something so horrible.

Grace took a deep breath as all eyes slowly turned to

look to the back of the aisle. The outdoor ceremony was the perfect setting for them. The property, the beautiful New England- style home was now theirs, the vast yard sweeping down to the river the only place she'd wanted to be married.

Dusk had settled and rows of gold Chiavari chairs had been laid out on the grass. Oversized white lanterns flanked each row, and a white runner led to the gazebo Evan had custom-built for today. The air smelled of spring blossoms and lilacs.

"Mommy, I think we're supposed to walk to Daddy now," Christopher whispered.

She smiled down at him and squeezed his hand. His little tuxedo made him look ever more the man, and she'd fought tears as she'd gotten him dressed for the wedding this afternoon.

They slowly walked down the aisle, toward the man that made them a whole family. He'd claimed Christopher as his and loved him unconditionally. Evan had made her dreams for Christopher come true.

As she passed faces of people that only a few months ago had been strangers, a warmth and sense of gratitude enveloped her. All these people, this town had swallowed her, taken her and Christopher in and given them what they'd always really wanted—a home. Grace's eyes were firmly locked on Evan's.

She clutched her bouquet of roses tightly as Evan gave her a slight smile. Her body came to life as his eyes wandered over her. He was breathtaking in his dark suit and white shirt, with a blue tie that only intensified the color of his eyes.

Evan Manning had rescued them once, he'd restored her faith, and he'd given them all of himself. He was the man in her sketchbook, in her heart, in her soul.

• • •

Evan smiled, blinking past the emotion that clouded his eyes as Grace and Christopher walked toward him. His entire family stood at the altar. Family. They were all his family. The people that he'd been so quick to dismiss at one point in his life, were now his entire life.

Jake's hand briefly touched his shoulder as Grace and Christopher appeared at the top of the aisle. Evan looked past the smiling faces of the guests, the pink and white flowers lining the aisle, Eunice Jacobs's bright orange hat, passed Dr. Chalmers, to the two people that encompassed his entire world. Grace's eyes were steady, locked on his, the love brimming from the emerald depths obvious even with the distance. She looked down at Christopher for a moment, who gave her a smile, and then they walked toward him. His son smiled at him and gave him a wave as he held Grace's hand and made their way down the aisle.

Jake leaned forward. "And here we are, at yet another wedding. What was it you said about Eunice's being the last wedding you'd ever attend with us?"

Evan grinned and turned his head to look at Jake. Today, he didn't need a smart-ass retort. He could give one, but he didn't need to. Today was all about Grace and Christopher and the new life they were officially starting.

Quinn slapped him on the back. "I knew the second those words came out of your mouth you were screwed."

He smiled as his brothers stepped back and Grace and Christopher stepped forward.

Evan knew that despite everything, all the times Grace claimed that he'd saved them, the young woman and child walking toward him had done the saving. They forced him to be the man he truly wanted to be. These people, this town, they were in his blood. He had no reason to run anymore and all the reasons to stay here forever.

Grace and Christopher finally stood in front of him, and he stepped down, grasping each of their hands in his.

"You look beautiful," he whispered in Grace's ear. She smiled up at him, and he knew. He knew he'd found his salvation in Grace.

# Acknowledgements

To Tracy, my editor:

Thank you for your endless patience, diligence, and enthusiasm. You truly understood Red River and all its quirky characters. It was such a joy to work with you!

Victoria

xo

# About the Author

Victoria James always knew she wanted to be a writer and in grade five, she penned her first story, bound it (with staples) and a cardboard cover and did all the illustrations herself. Luckily, this book will never see the light of day again.

In high school she fell in love with historical romance and then contemporary romance. After graduating University with an English Literature degree, Victoria married her own hero, pursued a degree in Interior Design and then opened her own business. After their first child, Victoria knew it was time to fulfill the dream of writing romantic fiction.

Victoria is a hopeless romantic who is living her dream, penning happily-ever-afters for her characters in between managing kids and the family business. Writing on a laptop in the middle of the country in a rambling old Victorian house would be ideal, but she's quite content living in suburbia with her husband, their two young children, and very bad cat.

Victoria loves connecting with readers, and you can find her online at www.victoriajames.ca and on Twitter @ vicjames101

*Also by Victoria James*

THE BEST MAN'S BABY
a Red River novel

A RISK WORTH TAKING
a Red River novel

THE RANCHER'S SECOND CHANCE
a Passion Creek novel

THE BILLIONAIRE'S CHRISTMAS BABY